THE PLEASURES OF

THE DAMNED

THE PLEASURES OF
THE DAMNED

POEMS, 1951–1993

. . . .

charles bukowski

edited by john martin

ecco

An Imprint of HarperCollins Publishers

HarperCollins books may be purchased for educational, business, or sales promotional use. For information, please e-mail the Special Markets Department at SPsales@harpercollins.com.

A hardcover edition of this book was published in 2007 by Ecco, an imprint of HarperCollins Publishers.

First Ecco paperback published 2008.

Designed by Cassandra J. Pappas
Frontispiece © Ulf Andersen / Gamma

Library of Congress Cataloging-in-Publication Data is available upon request.

ISBN 978-0-06-122844-5

23 24 25 26 27 LBC 30 29 28 27 26

contents

THE PLEASURES OF
THE DAMNED

the mockingbird

the mockingbird had been following the cat
all summer
mocking mocking mocking
teasing and cocksure;
the cat crawled under rockers on porches
tail flashing
and said something angry to the mockingbird
which I didn't understand.

yesterday the cat walked calmly up the driveway
with the mockingbird alive in its mouth,
wings fanned, beautiful wings fanned and flopping,
feathers parted like a woman's legs,
and the bird was no longer mocking,
it was asking, it was praying
but the cat
striding down through centuries
would not listen.

I saw it crawl under a yellow car
with the bird
to bargain it to another place.

summer was over.

something's knocking at the door

a great white light dawns across the
continent
as we fawn over our failed traditions,
often kill to preserve them
or sometimes kill just to kill.
it doesn't seem to matter: the answers dangle just
out of reach,
out of hand, out of mind.

the leaders of the past were insufficient,
the leaders of the present are unprepared.
we curl up tightly in our beds at night and wait.
it is a waiting without hope, more like
a prayer for unmerited grace.

it all looks more and more like the same old
movie.
the actors are different but the plot's the same:
senseless.

we should have known, watching our fathers.
we should have known, watching our mothers.
they did not know, they too were not prepared to
teach.
we were too naive to ignore their
counsel
and now we have embraced their
ignorance as our
own.
we are them, multiplied.
we are their unpaid debts.
we are bankrupt

in money and
in spirit.

there are a few exceptions, of course,
but these teeter on the
edge
and will
at any moment
tumble down to join the rest
of us,
the raving, the battered, the blind and the sadly
corrupt.

a great white light dawns across the
continent,
the flowers open blindly in the stinking wind,
as grotesque and ultimately
unlivable
our 21st century
struggles to be
born.

his wife, the painter

There are sketches on the walls of men and women and ducks,
and outside a large green bus swerves through traffic like
insanity sprung from a waving line; Turgenev, Turgenev,
says the radio, and Jane Austen, Jane Austen, too.

"I am going to do her portrait on the 28th, while you are at work."

He is just this edge of fat and he walks constantly, he
fritters; they have him; they are eating him hollow like
a webbed fly, and his eyes are red-suckled with anger-fear.

He feels the hatred and discard of the world, sharper than
his razor, and his gut-feel hangs like a wet polyp; and he
self-decisions himself defeated trying to shake his
hung beard from razor in water (like life), not warm enough.

*Daumier. Rue Transnonain, le 15 Avril, 1843. (Lithograph.) Paris,
Bibliothèque Nationale.*

"She has a face unlike that of any woman I have ever known."

"What is it? A love affair?"

"Silly. I can't love a woman. Besides, she's pregnant."

I can paint—a flower eaten by a snake; that sunlight is a
lie; and that markets smell of shoes and naked boys clothed,
and under everything some river, some beat, some twist that
clambers along the edge of my temple and bites nip-dizzy . . .
men drive cars and paint their houses,
but they are mad; men sit in barber chairs; buy hats.

Corot. Recollection of Mortefontaine.
Paris, Louvre

"I must write Kaiser, though I think he's a homosexual."

"Are you still reading Freud?"

"Page 299."

She made a little hat and he fastened two snaps under one
arm, reaching up from the bed like a long feeler from the
snail, and she went to church, and he thought now I h've
time and the dog.

About church: the trouble with a mask is it
never changes.

So rude the flowers that grow and do not grow beautiful.
So magic the chair on the patio that does not hold legs
and belly and arm and neck and mouth that bites into the
wind like the end of a tunnel.

He turned in bed and thought: I am searching for some
segment in the air. It floats about the people's heads.
When it rains on the trees it sits between the branches
warmer and more blood-real than the dove.

Orozco. Christ Destroying the Cross.
Hanover, Dartmouth College, Baker Library.

He burned away in sleep.

on the sidewalk and in the sun

I have seen an old man around town recently
carrying an enormous pack.
he uses a walking stick
and moves up and down the streets
with this pack strapped to his back.

I keep seeing him.

if he'd only throw that pack away, I think,
he'd have a chance, not much of a chance
but a chance.

and he's in a tough district—east Hollywood.
they aren't going to give him a
dry bone in east Hollywood.

he is lost. with that pack.
on the sidewalk and in the sun.

god almighty, old man, I think, throw away that
pack.

then I drive on, thinking of my own
problems.

the last time I saw him he was not walking.
it was ten thirty a.m. on north Bronson and
hot, very hot, and he sat on a little ledge, bent,
the pack still strapped to his back.

I slowed down to look at his face.
I had seen one or two other men in my life

with looks on their faces like
that.

I speeded up and turned on the
radio.

I knew that look.

I would never see him again.

the elephants of Vietnam

first they used to, he told me,
gun and bomb the elephants,
you could hear their screams over all the other sounds;
but you flew high to bomb the people,
you never saw it,
just a little flash from way up
but with the elephants
you could watch it happen
and hear how they screamed;
I'd tell my buddies, listen, you guys
stop that,
but they just laughed
as the elephants scattered
throwing up their trunks (if they weren't blown off)
opening their mouths
wide and
kicking their dumb clumsy legs
as blood ran out of big holes in their bellies.

then we'd fly back,
mission completed.
we'd get everything:
convoys, dumps, bridges, people, elephants and
all the rest.

he told me later, I
felt bad about the
elephants.

dark night poem

they say that
nothing is wasted:
either that
or
it all is.

(uncollected)

the last days of the suicide kid

I can see myself now
after all these suicide days and nights,
being wheeled out of one of those sterile rest homes
(of course, this is only if I get famous and lucky)
by a subnormal and bored nurse . . .
there I am sitting upright in my wheelchair . . .
almost blind, eyes rolling backward into the dark part of my skull
    looking
for the mercy of death . . .

"Isn't it a lovely day, Mr. Bukowski?"

"O, yeah, yeah . . ."

the children walk past and I don't even exist
and lovely women walk by
with big hot hips
and warm buttocks and tight hot everything
praying to be loved
and I don't even
exist . . .

"It's the first sunlight we've had in 3 days,
Mr. Bukowski."

"Oh, yeah, yeah."

there I am sitting upright in my wheelchair,
myself whiter than this sheet of paper,
bloodless,
brain gone, gamble gone, me, Bukowski,
gone . . .

"Isn't it a lovely day, Mr. Bukowski?"

"O, yeah, yeah . . ." pissing in my pajamas, slop drooling out of
    my mouth.

2 young schoolboys run by—

"Hey, did you see that old guy?"

"Christ, yes, he made me sick!"

after all the threats to do so
somebody else has committed suicide for me
at last.

the nurse stops the wheelchair, breaks a rose from a nearby bush,
    puts it in my hand.

I don't even know
what it is. it might as well be my pecker
for all the good
it does.

tabby cat

he has on blue jeans and tennis shoes
and walks with two young girls
about his age.
every now and then he leaps
into the air and
clicks his heels together.

he's like a young colt
but somehow he also reminds me
more of a tabby cat.

his ass is soft and
he has no more on his mind
than a gnat.

he jumps along behind his girls
clicking his heels together.

then he pulls the hair of one
runs over to the other and
squeezes her neck.

he has fucked both of them and
is pleased with himself.
it has all happened
so easily for him.

and I think, ah,
my little tabby cat
what nights and days
wait for you.

your soft ass
will be your doom.
your agony
will be endless
and the girls
who are yours now
will soon belong to other men
who didn't get their cookies
and cream so easily and
so early.

the girls are practicing on you
the girls are practicing for other men
for someone out of the jungle
for someone out of the lion cage.

I smile as
I watch you walking along
clicking your heels together.

my god, boy, I fear for you
on that night
when you first find out.

it's a sunny day now.

jump
while you
can.

metamorphosis

a girlfriend came in
built me a bed
scrubbed and waxed the kitchen floor
scrubbed the walls
vacuumed
cleaned the toilet
the bathtub
scrubbed the bathroom floor
and cut my toenails and
my hair.

then
all on the same day
the plumber came and fixed the kitchen faucet
and the toilet
and the gas man fixed the heater
and the phone man fixed the phone.
now I sit here in all this perfection.
it is quiet.
I have broken off with all 3 of my girlfriends.

I felt better when everything was in
disorder.
it will take me some months to get back to
normal:
I can't even find a roach to commune with.

I have lost my rhythm.
I can't sleep.
I can't eat.

I have been robbed of
my filth.

a poem is a city

a poem is a city filled with streets and sewers
filled with saints, heroes, beggars, madmen,
filled with banality and booze,
filled with rain and thunder and periods of
drought, a poem is a city at war,
a poem is a city asking a clock why,
a poem is a city burning,
a poem is a city under guns
its barbershops filled with cynical drunks,
a poem is a city where God rides naked
through the streets like Lady Godiva,
where dogs bark at night, and chase away
the flag; a poem is a city of poets,
most of them quite similar
and envious and bitter . . .
a poem is this city now,
50 miles from nowhere,
9:09 in the morning,
the taste of liquor and cigarettes,
no police, no lovers, walking the streets,
this poem, this city, closing its doors,
barricaded, almost empty,
mournful without tears, aging without pity,
the hardrock mountains,
the ocean like a lavender flame,
a moon destitute of greatness,
a small music from broken windows . . .

a poem is a city, a poem is a nation,
a poem is the world . . .

and now I stick this under glass
for the mad editor's scrutiny,
and night is elsewhere
and faint gray ladies stand in line,
dog follows dog to estuary,
the trumpets bring on gallows
as small men rant at things
they cannot do.

a smile to remember

we had goldfish and they circled around and around
in the bowl on the table near the heavy drapes
covering the picture window and
my mother, always smiling, wanting us all
to be happy, told me, "be happy, Henry!"
and she was right: it's better to be happy if you
can
but my father continued to beat her and me several times a week
    while
raging inside his 6-foot-2 frame because he couldn't
understand what was attacking him from within.

my mother, poor fish,
wanting to be happy, beaten two or three times a
week, telling me to be happy: "Henry, *smile*!
why don't you ever *smile*?"

and then she would smile, to show me how, and it was the
saddest smile I ever saw.

one day the goldfish died, all five of them,
they floated on the water, on their sides, their
eyes still open,
and when my father got home he threw them to the cat
there on the kitchen floor and we watched as my mother
smiled.

dying for a beer dying
for and of life
on a windy afternoon in Hollywood
listening to symphony music from my little red radio
on the floor.

a friend said,
"all ya gotta do is go out on the sidewalk
and lay down
somebody will pick you up
somebody will take care of you."

I look out the window at the sidewalk
I see something walking on the sidewalk
she wouldn't lay down there,
only in special places for special people with special $$$$
and
special ways
while I am dying for a beer on a windy afternoon in
Hollywood,
nothing like a beautiful broad dragging it past you on the
sidewalk
moving it past your famished window
she's dressed in the finest cloth
she doesn't care what you say
how you look what you do
as long as you do not get in her
way, and it must be that she doesn't shit or
have blood
she must be a cloud, friend, the way she floats past us.

I am too sick to lay down
the sidewalks frighten me
the whole damned city frightens me,
what I will become
what I have become
frightens me.

ah, the bravado is gone
the big run through center is gone
on a windy afternoon in Hollywood
my radio cracks and spits its dirty music
through a floor full of empty beerbottles.

now I hear a siren
it comes closer
the music stops
the man on the radio says,
"we will send you a free 25-page booklet:
FACE THE FACTS ABOUT COLLEGE COSTS."

the siren fades into the cardboard mountains
and I look out the window again as the clasped fist of
boiling cloud comes down—
the wind shakes the plants outside
I wait for evening I wait for night I wait sitting in a chair
by the window—
the cook drops in the live

red-pink salty
rough-tit crab and
the game works
on

come get me.

they, all of them, know

ask the sidewalk painters of Paris
ask the sunlight on a sleeping dog
ask the 3 pigs
ask the paperboy
ask the music of Donizetti
ask the barber
ask the murderer
ask the man leaning against a wall
ask the preacher
ask the maker of cabinets
ask the pickpocket or the
       pawnbroker or the glass blower
       or the seller of manure or
       the dentist
ask the revolutionist
ask the man who sticks his head in
       the mouth of a lion
ask the man who will release the next
       atom bomb
ask the man who thinks he's Christ
ask the bluebird who comes home
       at night
ask the peeping Tom
ask the man dying of cancer
ask the man who needs a bath
ask the man with one leg
ask the blind
ask the man with the lisp
ask the opium eater
ask the trembling surgeon
ask the leaves you walk upon

ask a rapist or a
    streetcar conductor or an old man
    pulling weeds in his garden
ask a bloodsucker
ask a trainer of fleas
ask a man who eats fire
ask the most miserable man you can
    find in his most
    miserable moment
ask a teacher of judo
ask a rider of elephants
ask a leper, a lifer, a lunger
ask a professor of history
ask the man who never cleans his
    fingernails
ask a clown or ask the first face you see
    in the light of day
ask your father
ask your son and
    his son to be
ask me
ask a burned-out bulb in a paper sack
ask the tempted, the damned, the foolish
    the wise, the slavering
ask the builders of temples
ask the men who have never worn shoes
ask Jesus
ask the moon
ask the shadows in the closet
ask the moth, the monk, the madman
ask the man who draws cartoons for
    The New Yorker

ask a goldfish
ask a fern shaking to a tapdance
ask the map of India
ask a kind face
ask the man hiding under your bed
ask the man you hate the most in this
    world
ask the man who drank with Dylan Thomas
ask the man who laced Jack Sharkey's gloves
ask the sad-faced man drinking coffee
ask the plumber
ask the man who dreams of ostriches every
    night
ask the ticket taker at a freak show
ask the counterfeiter
ask the man sleeping in an alley under
    a sheet of paper
ask the conquerors of nations and planets
ask the man who has just cut off his finger
ask a bookmark in the bible
ask the water dripping from a faucet while
    the phone rings
ask perjury
ask the deep blue paint
ask the parachute jumper
ask the man with the bellyache
ask the divine eye so sleek and swimming
ask the boy wearing tight pants in
    the expensive academy
ask the man who slipped in the bathtub
ask the man chewed by the shark

ask the one who sold me the unmatched
    gloves
ask these and all those I have left out
ask the fire the fire the fire—
ask even the liars
ask anybody you please at any time
      you please on any day you please
      whether it's raining or whether
      the snow is there or whether
      you are stepping out onto a porch
      yellow with warm heat
ask this ask that
ask the man with birdshit in his hair
ask the torturer of animals
ask the man who has seen many bullfights
    in Spain
ask the owners of new Cadillacs
ask the famous
ask the timid
ask the albino
    and the statesman
ask the landlords and the poolplayers
ask the phonies
ask the hired killers
ask the bald men and the fat men
    and the tall men and the
    short men
ask the one-eyed men, the
    oversexed and undersexed men
ask the men who read all the newspaper
    editorials
ask the men who breed roses

ask the men who feel almost no pain
ask the dying
ask the mowers of lawns and the attenders
    of football games
ask any of these or all of these
ask ask ask and
    they'll all tell you:

a snarling wife on the balustrade is more
than a man can bear.

a future congressman

in the men's room at the
track
this boy of about
7 or 8 years old
came out of a stall
and the man
waiting for him
(probably his father)
asked,
"what did you do with the
racing program?
I gave it to you
to keep."
"no," said the boy,
"I ain't seen it! I don't
have it!"

they walked off and
I went into the stall
because it was the only one
available
and there
in the toilet
was the
program.

I tried to flush
the program
away
but it just swam
sluggishly about

and
remained.

I got out of
there and found
another
empty stall.

that boy was ready
for his life to come,
he would undoubtedly
be highly successful,
the lying little
prick.

eulogy

with old cars, especially when you buy them second-
hand and drive them for many years
a love affair is inevitable:
you even learn to
accept their little
eccentricities:
the leaking water pump
the failing plugs
the rusted throttle arm
the reluctant carburetor
the oily engine
the dead clock
the frozen speedometer and
other sundry
defects.
you also learn all the tricks to
keep the love affair alive:
how to slam the glove compartment so that
it will stay closed,
how to slap the headlight with an open palm
in order to have
light,
how many times to pump the gas pedal
and how long to wait before
touching the starter,
and you overlook each burn hole in the
upholstery
and each spring
poking through the fabric.
your car has been in and out of
police impounds,
has been ticketed for various

malfunctions:
broken wipers,
no turn signals, missing
brake light, broken tail lights, bad
brakes, excessive
exhaust and so forth
but in spite of everything
you knew you were in good hands,
there was never an accident, the
old car moved you from one place to
another,
faithfully
—the poor man's miracle.
so when that last breakdown did occur,
when the valves quit,
when the tired pistons
cracked, or the
crankshaft failed and
you sold it for
junk
—you then had to watch it carted
away
hanging there
from the back of the tow truck
wheeled off
as if it had no
soul,
the bald rear tires
the cracked back window and
the twisted license plate
were the last things you
saw, and it

hurt
as if some woman you loved very
much
and lived with
year after year
had died
and now you
would never
again know
her music
her magic
her unbelievable
fidelity.

the drowning

for five years I have been looking
across the way
at the side of a red apartment house.
there must be people in there
even love in there
whatever that means.

here blows a horn, there sounds a
piano, and yesterday's newspapers are as
yellow as the grass.
five years.
a man can drown in five years,
while the red bricks
stand forever.

I hear sounds now like dancing in the
air
great bladders of blood are being loosed in
Mariposa Ave.
sweat drenches my temple like beads on a
cold beer can
as armies fight in my head.

I see a woman come out of the redbrick
apartment house.
she is fat and comfortable
the slow horse of her body moves
under a dress of pink carnations
playing tricks with my better sense
and now she is gone and
the bricks look back at me
the bricks with their

windows and the windows look at me
and a bird on a telephone wire looks
and I feel naked as I
try to forget all the good dead.

a band plays wildly
LOOKAWAY, LOOKAWAY,
DIXIELAND!
as they empty bladders of poison
and bags of oranges over Mariposa Ave.
and the cars run through them like poor snow
and my pink woman comes back and I
try to tell her
    wait! wait!
      don't go back in there!
but she goes inside as
my bird flies away
and it is just
another hot evening in
Los Angeles:
some bricks, a mongoose or two, Chimera and
disbelief.

(uncollected)

fooling Marie (the poem)

he met her at the racetrack, a strawberry
blonde with round hips, well-bosomed, long legs,
turned-up nose, flower mouth, in a pink dress,
wearing white high-heeled shoes.
she began asking him questions about various
horses while looking up at him with her pale blue
eyes.

he suggested the bar and they had a drink, then
watched the next race together.
he hit fifty-win on a sixty-to-one shot and she
jumped up and down.
then she whispered in his ear,
"you're the magic man! I want to fuck you!"
he grinned and said, "I'd like to, but
Marie . . . my wife . . ."
she laughed, "we'll go to a motel!"

so they cashed the ticket, went to the parking lot,
got into her car. "I'll drive you back when
we're finished," she smiled.

they found a motel about a mile
west. she parked, they got out, checked in, went to
room 302.
they had stopped for a bottle of Jack Daniel's
on the way. he stood and took the glasses out of the
cellophane. as she undressed he poured two.

she had a marvelous young body. she sat on the edge of
the bed sipping at the Jack Daniel's as he
undressed. he felt awkward, fat and old

but knew he was lucky: it promised to be his best day
ever.
then he too sat on the edge of the bed with her and
his Jack Daniel's. she reached over
and grabbed him between the legs, bent over
and went down on him.

he pulled her under the covers and they played some more.
finally, he mounted her and it was great, it was a
miracle, but soon it ended, and when she
went to the bathroom he poured two more drinks
thinking, I'll shower real good, Marie will never
know.

she came out and they sat in bed
making small talk.
"I'm going to shower now," he told her,
"I'll be out soon."

"o.k., cutie," she said.

he soaped good in the shower, washing away all the
perfume, the woman-smell.

"hurry up, daddy!" he heard her say.

"I won't be long, baby!" he yelled from the
shower.

he got out, toweled off, then opened the bathroom
door and stepped out.

the motel room was empty.
she was gone.

on some impulse he ran to the closet, pulled the door
open: nothing there but coat hangers.

then he noticed that his clothes were gone, his under-
wear, his shirt, his pants with the car keys and his wallet,
all the money, his shoes, his stockings, everything.

on another impulse he looked under the bed.
nothing.

then he saw the bottle of Jack Daniel's, half full,
standing on the dresser.
he walked over and poured a drink.
as he did he saw the word scrawled on the dresser
mirror in pink lipstick: SUCKER.

he drank the whiskey, put the glass down and watched himself
in the mirror, very fat, very tired, very old.
he had no idea what to do next.

he carried the whiskey, back to the bed, sat down,
lifted the bottle and sucked at it as the light from the
boulevard came in through the dusty blinds. then he just sat
and looked out and watched the cars, passing back and
forth.

the young man on the bus stop bench

he sits all day at the bus stop
at Sunset and Western
his sleeping bag beside him.
he's dirty.
nobody bothers him.
people leave him alone.
the police leave him alone.
he could be the 2nd coming of Christ
but I doubt it.
the soles of his shoes are completely
gone.
he just laces the tops on
and sits and watches traffic.

I remember my own youthful days
(although I traveled lighter)
they were similar:
park benches
street corners
tarpaper shacks in Georgia for
$1.25 a week
not wanting the skid row church
hand-outs
too crazy to apply for relief
daytimes spent laying in public parks
bugs in the grass biting
looking into the sky
little insects whirling above my head
the breathing of white air
just breathing and waiting.

life becomes difficult:
being ignored
and ignoring.
everything turns into white air
the head fills with white air
and as invisible women sit in rooms
with successful bright-eyed young men
conversing brilliantly about everything
your sex drive
vanishes and it really
doesn't matter.
you don't want food
you don't want shelter
you don't want anything.
sometimes you die
sometimes you don't.

as I drive past
the young man on the bus stop bench
I am comfortable in my automobile
I have money in two different banks
I own my own home
but he reminds me of my young self
and I want to help him
but I don't know what to do.

today when I drove past again
he was gone

I suppose finally the world wasn't
pleased with him being there.

the bench still sits there on the corner
advertising something.

for they had things to say

the canaries were there, and the lemon tree
and the old woman with warts;
and I was there, a child
and I touched the piano keys
as they talked—
but not too loudly
for they had things to say,
the three of them;
and I watched them cover the canaries at night
with flour sacks:
"so they can sleep, my dear."

I played the piano quietly
one note at a time,
the canaries under their sacks,
and there were pepper trees,
pepper trees brushing the roof like rain
and hanging outside the windows
like green rain,
and they talked, the three of them
sitting in a warm night's semicircle,
and the keys were black and white
and responded to my fingers
like the locked-in magic
of a waiting, grown-up world;
and now they're gone, the three of them
and I am old:
pirate feet have trod
the clean-thatched floors
of my soul,
and the canaries sing no more.

silly damned thing anyhow

we tried to hide it in the house so that the
neighbors wouldn't see.
it was difficult, sometimes we both had to
be gone at once and when we returned
there would be excreta and urine all
about.
it wouldn't toilet train
but it had the bluest eyes you ever
saw
and it ate everything we did
and we often watched tv together.

one evening we came home and it was
gone.
there was blood on the floor,
there was a trail of blood.
I followed it outside and into the garden
and there in the brush it was,
mutilated.
there was a sign hung about its severed
throat:
"we don't want things like this in our
neighborhood."

I walked to the garage for the shovel.
I told my wife, "don't come out here."
then I walked back with the shovel and
began digging.
I sensed
the faces watching me from behind
drawn blinds.

they had their neighborhood back,
a nice quiet neighborhood with green
lawns, palm trees, circular driveways, children,
churches, a supermarket, etc.

I dug into the earth.

upon reading an interview with a best-selling novelist in our metropolitan daily newspaper

he talks like he writes
and he has a face like a dove, untouched by
externals.
a little shiver of horror runs through me as I read
about
his comfortable assured success.
"I am going to write an important novel next year," he says.
next year?
I skip some paragraphs
but the interview goes on for two and one-half pages
more.
it's like milk spilled on a tablecloth, it's as soothing as
talcum powder, it's the bones of an eaten fish, it's a damp
stain on a faded necktie, it's a gathering hum.
this man is very fortunate that he is not standing
in line at a soup kitchen.
this man has no concept of failure because he is
paid so well for it.
I am lying on the bed, reading.
I drop the paper to the floor.
then I hear a sound.
it is a small fly buzzing.
I watch it flying, circling the room in an irregular
pattern.

life at last.

harbor freeway south

the dead dogs of nowhere bark
as you approach another
traffic accident.

3 cars
one standing on its
grill
the other 2 laying
on their sides
wheels turning slowly.

3 of them
at rest:
strange angles
in the dark.

it has just
happened.

I can see the still
bodies
inside.

these cars
scattered like toys
against the freeway
center
divider.

like spacecraft
they have landed
there

as you
drive past.

there's no
ambulance yet
no police
cars.

the rain began
15 minutes
ago.

things occur.

volcanoes are
1500 times more
powerful than
the first a-
bomb.

the dead dogs of
nowhere
those dogs keep
barking.

those cars
there like that.

obscene.
a dirty trick.

it's like
somebody dying
of a heart
attack
in a crowded
elevator

everybody
watching.

I finally
reach my street
pull into
the driveway.

park.
get out.

she meets me
halfway
to the door.

"I don't know
what to do,"
she says, "the
stove
went out."

schoolyards of forever

the schoolyard was a horror show: the bullies, the
freaks
the beatings up against the wire fence
our schoolmates watching
glad that they were not the victim;
we were beaten well and good
time after time
and afterwards were
followed
taunted all the way home where often
more beatings awaited us.

in the schoolyard the bullies ruled well,
and in the restrooms and
at the water fountains they
owned and disowned us at will
but in our own way we held strong
never begged for mercy
we took it straight on
silently
we were toughened by that horror
a horror that would later serve us in good stead
and then strangely
as we grew stronger and bolder
the bullies gradually began to back off.

grammar school
jr. high
high school
we grew up like odd neglected plants
gathering nourishment where we could

blossoming in time
and later when the bullies tried to befriend us
we turned them away.

then college
where under a new regime
the bullies melted almost entirely away
we became more and they became much less.

but there were new bullies now
the professors
who had to be taught the hard lessons we'd learned
we glowed madly
it was grand and easy
the coeds dismayed at our gamble
and our nerve
but we looked right through them
to the larger fight waiting out there.

then when we arrived *out there*
it was back up against the fence
new bullies once again
deeply entrenched by society
bosses and the like
who kept us in our place for decades to come
so we had to begin all over again
in the street
and in small rooms of madness
rooms that were always dim at noon
it lasted and lasted for years like that
but our former training enabled us to endure

and after what seemed like
an eternity
we finally found the tunnel at the end of the light.

it was a small enough victory
no songs of braggadocio because
we knew we had won very little from very little,
and that we had fought so hard to be free
just for the simple sweetness of it.

but even now we still can see the grade school janitor
with his broom
and sleeping face;
we can still see the little girls with their curls
their hair so carefully brushed and shining
in their freshly starched dresses;

see the faces of the teachers
fat folded forlorn;

hear the bell at recess;
see the grass and the baseball diamond;
see the volleyball court and its white net;
feel the sun always up and shining there
spilling down on us like the juice of a giant tangerine.

and we did not soon forget
Herbie Ashcroft
our principal tormentor
his fists as hard as rocks
as we crouched trapped against the steel fence
as we heard the sounds of automobiles passing but not stopping

and as the world went about doing what it does
we asked for no mercy
and we returned the next day and the next and the next
to our classes
the little girls looking so calm and secure
as they sat upright in their seats
in that room of blackboards and chalk
while we hung on grimly to our stubborn disdain
for all the horror and all the strife
and waited for something better
to come along and comfort us
in that never-to-be-forgotten
grammar school world.

in the lobby

I saw him sitting in a lobby chair
in the Patrick Hotel
dreaming of flying fish
and he said "hello friend
you're looking good.
me, I'm not so well,
they've plucked out my hair
taken my bowels
and the color in my eyes
has gone back into the sea."

I sat down and listened
to him breathe
his last.

a bit later the clerk came over
with his green eyeshade on
and then the clerk saw what I knew
but neither of us knew
what the old man knew.

the clerk stood there
almost surprised,
taken,
wondering where the old man had gone.

he began to shake like an ape
who'd had a banana taken from his hand.

and then there was a crowd
and the crowd looked at the old man

as if he were a freak
as if there was something wrong with him.

I got up and walked out of the lobby
I went outside on the sidewalk
and I walked along with the rest of them
bellies, feet, hair, eyes
everything moving and going
getting ready to go back to the beginning
or light a cigar.

and then somebody stepped on
the back of my heel
and I was angry enough to swear.

sex

I am driving down Wilton Avenue
when this girl of about 15
dressed in tight blue jeans
that grip her behind like two hands
steps out in front of my car
I stop to let her cross the street
and as I watch her contours waving
she looks directly through my windshield
at me
with purple eyes
and then blows
out of her mouth
the largest pink globe of
bubble gum
I have ever seen
while I am listening to Beethoven
on the car radio.
she enters a small grocery store
and is gone
and I am left with
Ludwig.

a clean, well-lighted place

the old fart, he used his literary reputation
to reel them in one at a time,
each younger than the last.
he liked to meet them for luncheon and
wine
and he'd talk and listen to them
talk.
whatever wife or girlfriend he had at the moment
was made to
understand that this sort of thing made him
feel "young again."
and when the luncheons became more
than luncheons
the young ladies vied to bed down with
this
literary
genius.
in between, he continued to write,
and late at night in his favorite bar
he liked to talk about writing and his amorous
adventures.
actually, he was just a drunk
who liked young ladies,
writing itself,
and talking about writing.
it wasn't a bad life.
it was certainly more interesting than
what most men were
doing.
at one time he was probably the
most famous writer in the
world.

many tried to write like he did
drink like he did
act like he did
but he was the original.
then life began to
catch up with him.
he began to age quickly.
his large bulk began to wither.
he was growing old
before his time.
finally it got to where he couldn't
write anymore,
"it just wouldn't come"
and the psychiatrists couldn't
do anything for him but only
made it worse.
then he took his own cure,
early one morning,
alone
just as his father had done
many years
before.

a writer who can't write any
more is dead
anyhow.
he knew that.
he knew that what he was
killing was already
dead.

and then the critics
and the hangers-on
and the publicists
and his heirs
moved in
like vultures.

something for the touts, the nuns, the grocery clerks and you . . .

we have everything and we have nothing
and some men do it in churches
and some men do it by tearing butterflies
in half
and some men do it in Palm Springs
laying it into butterblondes
with Cadillac souls
Cadillacs and butterflies
nothing and everything,
the face melting down to the last puff
in a cellar in Corpus Christi.
there's something for the touts, the nuns,
the grocery clerks and you . . .
something at 8 a.m., something in the library
something in the river,
everything and nothing.
in the slaughterhouse it comes running along
the ceiling on a hook, and you swing it—
one
    two
        three
and then you've got it, $200 worth of dead
meat, its bones against your bones
something and nothing.
it's always early enough to die and
it's always too late,
and the drill of blood in the basin white
it tells you nothing at all
and the gravediggers playing poker over
5 a.m. coffee, waiting for the grass

to dismiss the frost . . .
they tell you nothing at all.

we have everything and we have nothing—
days with glass edges and the impossible stink
of river moss—worse than shit;
checkerboard days of moves and countermoves,
fagged interest, with as much sense in defeat as
in victory; slow days like mules
humping it slagged and sullen and sun-glazed
up a road where a madman sits waiting among
blue jays and wrens netted in and sucked a flakey
gray.
good days too of wine and shouting, fights
in alleys, fat legs of women striving around
your bowels buried in moans,
the signs in bullrings like diamonds hollering
Mother Capri, violets coming out of the ground
telling you to forget the dead armies and the loves
that robbed you.
days when children say funny and brilliant things
like savages trying to send you a message through
their bodies while their bodies are still
alive enough to transmit and feel and run up
and down without locks and paychecks and
ideals and possessions and beetle-like
opinions.
days when you can cry all day long in
a green room with the door locked, days
when you can laugh at the breadman

because his legs are too long, days
of looking at hedges . . .

and nothing, and nothing. the days of
the bosses, yellow men
with bad breath and big feet, men
who look like frogs, hyenas, men who walk
as if melody had never been invented, men
who think it is intelligent to hire and fire and
profit, men with expensive wives they possess
like 60 acres of ground to be drilled
or shown off or to be walled away from
the incompetent, men who'd kill you
because they're crazy and justify it because
it's the law, men who stand in front of
windows 30 feet wide and see nothing,
men with luxury yachts who can sail around
the world and yet never get out of their vest
pockets, men like snails, men like eels, men
like slugs, and not as good . . .

and nothing. getting your last paycheck
at a harbor, at a factory, at a hospital, at an
aircraft plant, at a penny arcade, at a
barbershop, at a job you didn't want
anyway.
income tax, sickness, servility, broken
arms, broken heads—all the stuffing
come out like an old pillow.

we have everything and we have nothing.
some do it well enough for a while and
then give way. fame gets them or disgust
or age or lack of proper diet or ink
across the eyes or children in college
or new cars or broken backs while skiing
in Switzerland or new politics or new wives
or just natural change and decay—
the man you knew yesterday hooking
for ten rounds or drinking for three days and
three nights by the Sawtooth mountains now
just something under a sheet or a cross
or a stone or under an easy delusion,
or packing a bible or a golf bag or a
briefcase: how they go, how they go!—all
the ones you thought would never go.

days like this. like your day today.
maybe the rain on the window trying to
get through to you. what do you see today?
what is it? where are you? the best
days are sometimes the first, sometimes
the middle and even sometimes the last.
the vacant lots are not bad, churches in
Europe on postcards are not bad. people in
wax museums frozen into their best sterility
are not bad, horrible but not bad. the
cannon, think of the cannon. and toast for
breakfast the coffee hot enough you

know your tongue is still there. three
geraniums outside a window, trying to be
red and trying to be pink and trying to be
geraniums. no wonder sometimes the women
cry, no wonder the mules don't want
to go up the hill. are you in a hotel room
in Detroit looking for a cigarette? one more
good day. a little bit of it. and as
the nurses come out of the building after
their shift, having had enough, eight nurses
with different names and different places
to go—walking across the lawn, some of them
want cocoa and a paper, some of them want a
hot bath, some of them want a man, some
of them are hardly thinking at all. enough
and not enough. arcs and pilgrims, oranges,
gutters, ferns, antibodies, boxes of
tissue paper.

in the most decent sometimes sun
there is the softsmoke feeling from urns
and the canned sound of old battleplanes
and if you go inside and run your finger
along the window ledge you'll find
dirt, maybe even earth.
and if you look out the window
there will be the day, and as you
get older you'll keep looking
keep looking

sucking your tongue in a little
ah ah   no no   maybe

some do it naturally
some obscenely
everywhere.

blue beads and bones

as the orchid dies
and the grass goes
insane, let's have one for the lost:

I met an old man
and a tired whore
in a bar
at 8:00 in the morning
across from MacArthur Park—
we were sitting over our beers
he and I and the old whore
who had slept in an unlocked car
the night before
and wore a blue necklace.
the old guy said to me:
"look at my arms. I'm all bone.
no meat on me."
and he pulled back his sleeves
and he was right—
bone with just a layer of skin
hanging like paper.
he said, "I don't eat
nothin'."
I bought him a beer and the
whore a beer.
now there, I thought, is a man
who doesn't eat
meat, he doesn't eat
vegetables. kind of a saint.
it was like a church in there
as only the truly lost
sit in bars on Tuesday mornings

at 8:00 a.m.
then the whore said, "Jesus,
if I don't score tonight I'm
finished. I'm scared, I'm really
scared. you guys can go to skid row
when things get bad. but where can a
woman go?"
we couldn't answer her.
she picked up her beer with one hand
and played with her blue beads with the
other.
I finished my beer, went to the
corner and got a Racing Form from Teddy the
newsboy—age 61.
"you got a hot one today?"
"no, Teddy, I gotta see the board; money
makes them run."
"I'll give you 4 bucks. bet one for
me."
I took his 4 bucks. that would buy a sandwich,
pay parking, plus 2
coffees. I got into my car, drove
off. too early for the
track. blue beads and bones. the
universe was
bent. a cop rode his bike right up
behind me. the day had really
begun.

like a cherry seed in the throat

naked in that bright
light
the four horse falls
and throws a 112-pound
boy into the hooves
of 35,000 eyes.

good night, sweet
little
motherfucker.

turnabout

she drives into the parking lot while
I am leaning up against the fender of my car.
she's drunk and her eyes are wet with tears:
"you son of a bitch, you fucked me when you
didn't want to. you told me to keep phoning
you, you told me to move closer into town,
then you told me to leave you alone."

it's all quite dramatic and I enjoy it.
"sure, well, what do you want?"

"I want to talk to you, I want to go to your
place and talk to you . . ."

"I'm with somebody now. she's in getting a
sandwich."

"I want to talk to you . . . it takes a while
to get over things. I need more time."

"sure. wait until she comes out. we're not
inhuman. we'll all have a drink together."

"shit," she says, "oh shit!"

she jumps into her car and drives off.

the other one comes out: "who was that?"

"an ex-friend."

now *she's* gone and I'm sitting here drunk
and my eyes seem wet with tears.

it's very quiet and I feel like I have a spear
rammed into the center of my gut.

I walk to the bathroom and puke.

mercy, I think, doesn't the human race know anything
about mercy?

mystery leg

first of all, I had a hard time, a very hard time
locating the parking lot for the building.
it wasn't off the main boulevard where
the cars all driven by merciless killers
were doing 55 mph in a 25 mph zone.
the man riding my bumper so
close I could see his snarling face
in my rearview mirror caused me
to miss the narrow alley that would have
allowed me to circle the west
end of the building in search of parking.
I went to the next street, took a right, then
took another right, spotted the building, a blue
heartless-looking structure, then took
another right and finally saw it, a tiny
sign: *parking*.
I drove in.
the guard had the wooden red and white
barrier down.
he stuck his head out a little window.
"yeah?" he asked.
he looked like a retired hit man.
"to see Dr. Manx," I said.
he looked at me disdainfully, then said,
"go ahead!"
the red and white barrier lifted.
I drove in,
drove around and around.
I finally found a parking spot a good distance away,
a football field away.
I walked in.
I finally found the entrance and the elevator

and the floor
and then the office number.
I walked in.
the waiting room was full.
there was an old lady talking to the
receptionist.
"but can't I see him now?"
"Mrs. Miller, you are here at the right time
but on the wrong day.
this is Wednesday, you'll have to come
back Friday."
"but I took a cab. I'm an old lady, I have almost
no money, can't I see him now?"
"Mrs. Miller, I'm sorry but your appointment
is on Friday, you'll have to come back
then."
Mrs. Miller turned away: unwanted,
old and poor, she walked to the
door.
I stepped up smartly, informed them who I was.
I was told to sit down and wait.
I sat with the others.
then I noticed the magazine rack.
I walked over and looked at the magazines.
it was odd: they weren't of recent
vintage: in fact, all of them were over a
year old.
I sat back down.
30 minutes passed.
45 minutes passed.
an hour passed.
the man next to me spoke:

"I've been waiting an hour and a half," he
said.
"that's hell," I said, "they shouldn't do that!"
he didn't reply.
just then the receptionist called my
name.
I got up and told her that the other man had
been waiting an hour and a half.
she acted as if she hadn't heard.
"please follow me," she said.
I followed her down a dark hall, then she
opened a door, pointed. "in there," she said.
I walked in and she closed the door behind me.
I sat down and looked at a map of
the human body hanging from the wall.
I could see the veins, the heart, the
intestines, all that.
it was cold in there and dark, darker
than in the hall.
I waited maybe 15 minutes before the door
opened.
it was Dr. Manx.
he was followed by a tired-looking young lady
in a white gown; she held a clipboard;
she looked depressed.
"well, now," said Dr. Manx, "what is it?"
"it's my leg," I said.
I saw the lady writing on the clipboard.
she wrote LEG.
"what is it about the leg?" asked the Dr.
"it hurts," I said.
PAIN wrote the lady.

then she saw me looking at the clipboard and
turned away.
"did you fill out the form they gave you at
the desk?" the Dr. asked.
"they didn't give me a form," I said.
"Florence," he said, "give him a form."
Florence pulled a form out from her
clipboard, handed it to me.
"fill that out," said Dr. Manx, "we'll be right
back."
then they were gone and I worked at the
form.
it was the usual: name, address, phone,
employer, relatives, etc.
there was also a long list of questions.
I marked them all "no."
then I sat there.
20 minutes passed.
then they were back.
the doctor began twisting my leg.
"it's the *right* leg," I said.
"oh," he said.
Florence wrote something on her
clipboard.
probably RIGHT LEG.
he switched to the right leg.
"does that hurt?"
"a little."
"not real bad?"
"no."
"does *this* hurt?"
"a little."

"not real bad?"
"well, the whole leg hurts but when
you do that, it hurts more."
"but not *real* bad?"
"what's real bad?"
"like you can't stand on it."
"I can stand on it."
"hmmm . . . stand up!"
"all right."
"now, rock on your toes, back and
forth, back and forth."
I did.
"hurt real bad?" he asked.
"just medium."
"you know what?" Dr. Manx asked.
"no."
"we've got a Mystery Leg here!"
Florence wrote something on the
clipboard.
"I have?"
"yes, I don't know yet what's wrong with
it.
I want you to come back in 30 days."
"30 days?"
"yes, and stop at the desk on your
way out, see the girl."
then they walked out.

at the checkout desk there was a long
row of bottles waiting, white bottles with
bright orange labels.
the girl at the desk looked at me.

"take 4 of those bottles."
I did.
she didn't offer me a bag so I stuck
them in my pockets.
"that'll be $143," she said.
"$143?" I asked.
"it's for the pills," she said.
I pulled out my credit card.
"oh, we don't take credit cards," she told
me.
"but I don't have that much money on
me."
"how much do you have?"
I looked in my wallet.
"23 dollars."
"we'll take that and bill you for the
rest."
I handed her the money.
"see you in 30 days," she smiled.
I walked out and into the waiting room.
the man who had been waiting an hour and
a half was still there.
I walked out into the hall, found the
elevator.
then I was on the first floor and out
into the parking lot.
my car was still a football field
away
and my right leg began to hurt like hell,
after all that twisting Dr.
Manx had done to it.
I moved slowly to my car, got in.

it started and soon I was out on the
boulevard again.
the 4 bottles of pills bulged painfully in my
pockets as I drove along.
now I only had one problem left, I had
to tell my wife
I had a Mystery Leg.
I could hear her already:
"what? you mean he couldn't tell
you what was *wrong* with your
leg?
what do you *mean*, he didn't
know?
and what are those PILLS?
here, let me see those!"

as I drove along, I switched on the
radio in search of some soothing
music.

there wasn't any.

the girl outside the supermarket

a very tall girl lifts her nose at me
outside a supermarket
as if I were a walking garbage
can; and I had no desire for her,
no more desire
than for a
phone pole.
what was her message?
that I would never see the top of her
pantyhose?

I am a man in his 50s
sex is no longer an aching mystery
to me, so I can't understand
being snubbed by a
phone pole.
I'll leave young girls to young
men.

it's a lonely world
of frightened people,
just as it has always
been.

(uncollected)

it is not much

I suppose like others
I have come through fire and sword,
love gone wrong,
head-on crashes, drunk at sea,
and I have listened to the simple sound of water running
in tubs
and wished to drown
but simply couldn't bear the others
carrying my body down three flights of stairs
to the round mouths of curious biddies;
the psyche has been burned
and left us senseless,
the world has been darker than lights out
in a closet full of hungry bats,
and the whiskey and wine entered our veins
when blood was too weak to carry on;
and it will happen to others,
and our few good times will be rare
because we have a critical sense
and are not easy to fool with laughter;
small gnats crawl our screen
but we see through
to a wasted landscape
and let them have their moment;
we only asked for leopards to guard
our thinning dreams.
I once lay in a
white hospital
for the dying and the dying
self, where some god pissed a rain of
reason to make things grow
only to die, where on my knees

I prayed for LIGHT,
I prayed for 1*i*g*h*t,
and praying
crawled like a blind slug into the
web
where threads of wind stuck against my mind
and I died of pity
for Man, for myself,
on a cross without nails,
watching in fear as
the pig belches in his sty, farts,
blinks and eats.

2 Outside, As Bones Break
in My Kitchen

they get up on their garage roof
both of them 80 or 90 years old
standing on the slant
she wanting to fall really
all the way
but hacking at the old roofing
with a hoe

and he
more coward
on his knees praying for more days
gluing chunks of tar
his ear listening
for more green rain
more green rain
and he says
mama be careful

and she says nothing
and hacks a hole
where a tulip
never grew.

The Japanese Wife

O lord, he said, Japanese women,
real women, they have not forgotten,
bowing and smiling
closing the wounds men have made;
but American women will kill you like they
tear a lampshade,
American women care less than a dime,
they've gotten derailed,
they're too nervous to make good:
always scowling, belly-aching,
disillusioned, overwrought;
but oh lord, say, the Japanese women:
there was this one,
I came home and the door was locked
and when I broke in she broke out the bread knife
and chased me under the bed
and her sister came
and they kept me under that bed for two days,
and when I came out, at last,
she didn't mention attorneys,
just said, you will never wrong me again,
and I didn't; but she died on me,
and dying, said, you can wrong me now,
and I did,
but you know, I felt worse then
than when she was living;
there was no voice, no knife,
nothing but little Japanese prints on the wall,
all those tiny people sitting by red rivers
with flying green birds,
and I took them down and put them face down
in a drawer with my shirts,

and it was the first time I realized
that she was dead, even though I buried her;
and some day I'll take them all out again,
all the tan-faced little people
sitting happily by their bridges and huts
and mountains—
but not right now,
not just yet.

the harder you try

the waste of words
continues with a stunning
persistence
as the waiter runs by carrying the loaded
tray
for all the wise white boys who laugh at
us.
no matter. no matter,
as long as your shoes are tied and
nobody is walking too close
behind.
just being able to scratch yourself and
be nonchalant is victory
enough.
those constipated minds that seek
larger meaning
will be dispatched with the other
garbage.
back off.
if there is light
it will find
you.

the lady in red

people went into vacant lots and pulled up greens to cook and the
men rolled Bull Durham or smoked Wings (10¢ a pack) and the dogs
were thin and the cats were thin and the cats learned how to catch
mice and rats and the dogs caught and killed the cats (some of the
cats), and gophers tore up the earth and people killed them by
attaching garden hoses to the exhaust pipes of their cars and
sticking the hoses into the gopher holes and when the gophers came
out the cats and the dogs and the people were afraid of them, they
circled and showed their long thin teeth, then they stopped and
shivered and as they did the cats rushed in followed by the dogs.
people raised chickens in their back yards and the roosters were
weak and the hens were thin and the people ate them if they didn't
lay eggs fast enough, and the best time of all was when John
Dillinger escaped from jail, and one of the saddest times of all was
when the Lady in Red fingered him and he was gunned down
coming out of that movie.
Pretty Boy Floyd, Baby Face Nelson, Machine Gun Kelly, Ma
Barker, Alvin Karpis, we loved them all. and there were always
wars starting in China and they never lasted long but the
newspapers had big black headlines: WAR IN CHINA!
the '30s were a time when people had very little and there was
nothing to hide behind, and that Bull Durham tag dangling from
the string coming out of your pocket—that showed you had it, you
could roll with one hand—plenty of time to practice and if somebody
looked at you wrong or said something you didn't like you cracked
him one right in the mouth. it was a glorious non-bullshit time,
especially after we got rid of Herbert Hoover.

the shower

we like to shower afterwards
(I like the water hotter than she)
and her face is always soft and peaceful
and she'll wash me first
spread the soap over my balls
lift the balls
squeeze them,
then wash the cock:
"hey, this thing is still hard!"
then get all the hair down there,—
the belly, the back, the neck, the legs,
I grin grin grin,
and then I wash her . . .
first the cunt, I
stand behind her, my cock in the cheeks of her ass
I gently soap up the cunt hairs,
wash there with a soothing motion,
I linger perhaps longer than necessary,
then I get the backs of the legs, the ass,
the back, the neck, I turn her, kiss her,
soap up the breasts, get them and the belly, the neck,
the fronts of the legs, the ankles, the feet,
and then the cunt, once more, for luck . . .
another kiss, and she gets out first,
toweling, sometimes singing while I stay in
turn the water on hotter
feeling the good times of love's miracle
I then get out . . .
it is usually mid-afternoon and quiet,
and getting dressed we talk about what else
there might be to do,
but being together solves most of it,

in fact, solves all of it
for as long as those things stay solved
in the history of woman and
man, it's different for each
better and worse for each—
for me, it's splendid enough to remember
past the marching of armies
and the horses that walk the streets outside
past the memories of pain and defeat and unhappiness:
Linda, you brought it to me,
when you take it away
do it slowly and easily
make it as if I were dying in my sleep instead of in
my life, amen.

i was glad

I was glad I had money in the Savings and Loan
Friday afternoon hungover
I didn't have a job

I was glad I had money in the Savings and Loan
I didn't know how to play a guitar
Friday afternoon hungover

Friday afternoon hungover
across the street from Norm's
across the street from The Red Fez

I was glad I had money in the Savings and Loan
split with my girlfriend and blue and demented
I was glad to have my passbook and stand in line

I watched the buses run up Vermont
I was too crazy to get a job as a driver of buses
and I didn't even look at the young girls

I got dizzy standing in line but I
just kept thinking I have money in this building
Friday afternoon hungover

I didn't know how to play the piano
or even hustle a damnfool job in a carwash
I was glad I had money in the Savings and Loan

finally I was at the window
it was my Japanese girl
she smiled at me as if I were some amazing god

back again, eh? she said and laughed
as I showed her my withdrawal slip and my passbook
as the buses ran up and down Vermont

the camels trotted across the Sahara
she gave me the money and I took the money
Friday afternoon hungover

I walked into the market and got a cart
and I threw sausages and eggs and bacon and bread in there
I threw beer and salami and relish and pickles and mustard in there

I looked at the young housewives wiggling casually
I threw t-bone steaks and porterhouse and cube steaks in my cart
and tomatoes and cucumbers and oranges in my cart

Friday afternoon hungover
split with my girlfriend and blue and demented
I was glad I had money in the Savings and Loan.

the angel who pushed his wheelchair

long ago he edited a little magazine
it was up in San Francisco
during the beat era
during the reading-poetry-with-jazz experiments
and I remember him because he never returned my manuscripts
even though I wrote him many letters,
humble letters, sane letters, and, at last, violent letters;
I'm told he jumped off a roof
because a woman wouldn't love him.
no matter. when I saw him again
he was in a wheelchair and carried a wine bottle to piss in;
he wrote very delicate poetry
that I, naturally, couldn't understand;
he autographed his book for me
(which he said I wouldn't like)
and once at a party I threatened to punch him and
I was drunk and he wept and
I took pity and instead hit the next poet who walked by
on the head with his piss bottle; so,
we had an understanding after all.

he had this very thin and intense woman
pushing him about, she was his arms and legs and
maybe for a while
his heart.
it was almost commonplace
at poetry readings where he was scheduled to read
to see her swiftly rolling him in,
sometimes stopping by me, saying,
"I don't see *how* we are going to get him up on the stage!"
sometimes she did. often she did.

then *she* began writing poetry, I didn't see much of it,
but, somehow, I was glad for her.
then she injured her neck while doing her yoga
and she went on disability, and again I was glad for her,
all the poets wanted to get disability insurance
it was better than immortality.

I met her in the market one day
in the bread section, and she held my hands and
trembled all over
and I wondered if they ever had sex
those two. well, they had the muse anyhow
and she told me she was writing poetry and articles
but really more poetry, she was really writing a lot,
and that's the last I saw of her
until one night somebody told me she'd o.d.'d
and I said, no, not her
and they said, yes, her.

it was a day or so later
sometime in the afternoon
I had to go to the Los Feliz post office
to mail some dirty stories to a sex mag.
coming back
outside a church
I saw these smiling creatures
so many of them smiling
the men with beards and long hair and wearing
blue jeans
and most of the women blonde
with sunken cheeks and tiny grins,

and I thought, ah, a wedding,
a nice old-fashioned wedding,
and then I saw him on the sidewalk
in his wheelchair
tragic yet somehow calm
looking grayer, a profile like a tamed hawk,
and I knew it was her funeral,
she had really o.d.'d
and he did look tragic out there.

I *do* have feelings, you know.

maybe tonight I'll try to read his book.

a time to remember

at North Avenue 21 drunk tank you slept on the floor and at night
there was always some guy who would step on your face on his
way to the crapper
and then you would curse him good, set him straight, so that
he would know enough to either be more careful or to
just lay there and hold it.

there was a large hill in back dense with foliage
you could see it through the barred window
and a few of the guys after being released would not go back to
skid row, they'd just walk up into that green hill where
they lived like animals.
part of it was a campground and some lived out of the
trash cans while others trekked back to skid row for meals but then
returned
and they all sold their blood each week for
wine.

there must have been 18 or 20 of them up there and
they were more or less just as happy as corporate lawyers
stockbrokers or airline
pilots.

civilization is divided into parts, like an orange, and when you
peel the skin off, pull the sections apart, chew it, the
final result is a mouthful of pale pulp which you can either
swallow or spit
out.

some just swallow it
like the guys down at North Avenue
21.

the wrong way

luxury ocean liners
crossing the water
full of the indolent
and rich
passing from this place to that
with their hearts gone
and their guts empty
like Xmas turkeys
the great blue sky above
wasted
all that water
wasted
all those
fingers, heads, toes, buttocks,
eyes, ears, legs, feet
asleep in
their American Express Card
staterooms.

it's like a floating tomb
going nowhere.

these are the floating dead.

yet the dead are not ugly
but the near-dead surely
are
most
surely are.

when do they laugh?
what do they think about
love?

what are they
doing
midst all that water?
and where do they seek
to go?

no wonder

Tony phoned and told me that
Jan had left him but that he was all right;
it helped him he said to think about other great men
like D. H. Lawrence
pissed off with life in general but still
milking his cow;
or to think about
T. Dreiser with his masses of copious
notes
painfully constructing his novels which then made
the very walls applaud;
or I think about van Gogh, Tony continued, a madman
who continued to make great paintings as the
village children threw rocks at his
window;
or, there was Harry Crosby and his mistress
in that fancy hotel room, dying together, swallowed by
the Black Sun;
or, take Tchaikovsky, that homo, marrying a
female opera singer and then standing in a freezing
river hoping to catch pneumonia while she went mad;
or Dos Passos, after all those left-wing books,
putting on a suit and a necktie and voting Republican;
or that homo Lorca, shot dead in the road, supposedly
for his politics but really because the mayor of that
town thought his wife had the hots for the poet;
or that other homo Crane, jumping over the rail of the boat
and into the propellor because while drunk he had
promised to marry some woman;
or Dostoyevsky crucified on the roulette wheel with
Christ on his mind;
or Hemingway, getting his ass kicked by Callaghan

(but Hem was correct in maintaining that F.
Scott couldn't write);
or sometimes, Tony continued, I remember that guy
with syphilis who went mad and just kept rowing in
circles on some lake—a Frenchman—anyhow, he
wrote great short stories . . .

listen, I asked, you gonna be all
right?

sure, sure, he answered, just thought I'd phone, good
night.

and he hung up
and I hung up, thinking Jesus
Christ no wonder Jan left
him.

a threat to my immortality

she undressed in front of me
keeping her pussy to the front
while I lay in bed with a bottle of
beer.

where'd you get that wart on
your ass? I asked.

that's no wart, she said,
that's a mole, a kind of
birthmark.

that thing scares me, I said,
let's call
it off.

I got out of bed and
walked into the other room and
sat on the rocker
and rocked.

she walked out. now, listen, you
old fart. you've got warts and scars and
all kinds of things all over
you. I do believe you're the ugliest
old man
I've ever seen.

forget that, I said, tell me some more
about that
mole on your butt.

she walked into the other room
and got dressed and then ran past me
slammed the door
and was
gone.

and to think,
she'd read all my books of
poetry too.

I just hoped she wouldn't tell
anybody that
I wasn't pretty.

my telephone

the telephone has not been kind of late,
of late there have been more and more calls
from people who want to come over and talk
from people who are depressed
from people who are lonely
from people who just don't know what to do
with their time;
I'm no snob, I try to help, try to suggest something that
might be of assistance
but there have been more calls
more and more calls
and what the callers don't realize is that
I too have
problems
and even when I don't
it's
necessary for me
sometimes
just to be alone and quiet and
doing nothing.
so the other day
after many days of listening to depressed and lonely people
wanting me to assuage their grief,
I was lying there
enjoying looking at the ceiling
when the phone rang
and I picked it up and said,
"listen, whatever your problem is or whatever it is you want,
I can't help you."
after a moment of silence
whoever it was hung up
and I felt like a man who had escaped.

I napped then, perhaps an hour, when the phone rang
again and I picked it up:
"whatever your problem is
I can't help you!"

"is this Mr. Chinaski?"

"yes."

"this is Helen at your dentist's
office to remind you
that you have an appointment at
3:30 tomorrow
afternoon."

I told her I'd be
there for her.

Carson McCullers

she died of alcoholism
wrapped in a blanket
on a deck chair
on an ocean
steamer.

all her books of
terrified loneliness

all her books about
the cruelty
of loveless love

were all that was left
of her

as the strolling vacationer
discovered her body

notified the captain

and she was quickly dispatched
to somewhere else
on the ship

as everything
continued just
as
she had written it.

Mongolian coasts shining in light

Mongolian coasts shining in light,
I listen to the pulse of the sun,
the tiger is the same to all of us
and high   oh
so high on the branch
our oriole
sings.

putrefaction

of late
I've had this thought
that this country
has gone backwards
4 or 5 decades
and that all the
social advancement
the good feeling of
person toward
person
has been washed
away
and replaced by the same
old
bigotries.

we have
more than ever
the selfish wants of power
the disregard for the
weak
the old
the impoverished
the
helpless.

we are replacing want with
war
salvation with
slavery.

we have wasted the
gains

we have become
rapidly
less.

we have our Bomb
it is our fear
our damnation
and our
shame.

now
something so sad
has hold of us
that
the breath
leaves
and we can't even
cry.

where was Jane?

one of the first actors to play Tarzan was living at the
Motion Picture Home.
he'd been there for years waiting to die.
he spent much of his time
running in and out of the wards
into the cafeteria and out into the yard where he'd yell,
"ME TARZAN!"
he never spoke to anyone or said anything else, it was always just
"ME TARZAN!"
everybody liked him: the old actors, the retired directors,
the ancient script writers, the aged cameramen, the prop men,
     stunt men, the old
actresses, all of whom were also there
waiting to die; they enjoyed his verve,
his antics, he was harmless and he took them back to the time
     when they
were still in the business.

then the doctors in authority decided that Tarzan was possibly
     dangerous
and one day he was shipped off to a mental institution.
he vanished as suddenly as if he'd been eaten by a
lion.
and the other patients were outraged, they instituted legal
     proceedings
to have him returned at once but
it took some months.

when Tarzan returned he was changed.
he would not leave his room.
he just sat by the window as if he had
forgotten

his old role
and the other patients missed
his antics, his verve, and
they too felt somehow defeated and
diminished.
they complained about the change in Tarzan
doped and drugged in his room
and they knew he would soon die like that
and then he did
and then he was back in that other jungle
(to where we will all someday retire)
unleashing the joyful primal call they could no longer
hear.

there were some small notices in the
newspapers
and the paint continued to chip from the hospital
walls,
many plants died, there was an unfortunate
suicide,
a growing lack of trust and
hope, and
a pervasive sadness:
it wasn't so much Tarzan's death the others mourned,
it was the cold, willful attitude of the
young and powerful doctors
despite the wishes of the
helpless old.

and finally they knew the truth
while sitting in their rooms
that it wasn't only the attitude of the doctors

they had to fear,
and that as silly as all those Tarzan films had been,
and as much as they would miss their own lost
Tarzan,
that all that was much kinder than the final vigil
they would now have to sit and patiently endure
alone.

something about a woman

ah, Merryman,
a fighter on the docks,
killed a man while they were unloading
bananas.
I mean the man he killed
clubbed him first
from behind
with an anchor chain
(something about a woman)
and we all circled around
while
Merryman
did him in
under a hard-on sun,
finally strangling him to death
throwing him into the
ocean.
Merryman leaped to the dock
and walked
away, nobody tried to stop
him.
then we went back to work and
unloaded the rest of the bananas.
nothing was ever said about the murder
between any of us
and I never saw anything about it
in the papers.
although I saw some of the bananas
later in the

markets:
2 lbs. for a quarter
they seemed a
bargain.

(uncollected)

Sunday lunch at the Holy Mission

he got knifed in broad daylight, came up the street
holding his hands over his gut, dripping red
on the pavement.
nobody waiting in line left their place to help him.
he made it to the Mission doorway, collapsed in the
lobby where the desk clerk screamed, "hey, you
son-of-a-bitch, what are you doing?"
then he called an ambulance but the man was dead
when they got there.
the police came and circled the spots of blood
on the pavement
with white chalk
photographed everything
then asked the men waiting for their Sunday meal
if they had seen anything
if they knew anything.
they all said "no" to both.

while the police strutted in their uniforms
the others finally loaded the body into an ambulance.

afterwards the homeless men rolled cigarettes
as they waited for their meal
talking about the action
blowing farts and smoke
enjoying the sun
feeling quite like
celebrities.

trashcan lives

the wind blows hard tonight
and it's a cold wind
and I think about
the boys on the row.
I hope some of them have a bottle
of red.

it's when you're on the row
that you notice that
everything
is owned
and that there are locks on
everything.
this is the way a democracy
works:
you get what you can,
try to keep that
and add to it
if possible.

this is the way a dictatorship
works too
only they either enslave or
destroy their
derelicts.

we just forget
ours.

in either case
it's a hard
cold
wind.

school days

I'm in bed.
it's morning
and I hear:
where are your socks?
please get dressed!
why does it take you so long to
get dressed?
where's the brush?
all right, I'll give you a head
band!
what time is it?
where's the clock?
where did you put the clock?
aren't you dressed yet?
where's the brush?
where's your sandwich?
did you make a sandwich?
I'll make your sandwich.
honey and peanut butter.
and an orange.
there.
where's the brush?
I'll use a comb.
all right, holler. you lost the brush!
where did you lose the brush?
all right. now isn't that better?
where's your coat?
go find your coat.
your coat has to be around somewhere!
listen, what are you doing?
what are you playing with?
now you've spilled it all!

I hear them open the door
go down the stairway,
get into the car.
I hear them drive away. they are gone,
down the hill
on the way to
nursery school.

grass

at the window
I watch a man with a
power mower
the sounds of his doing race like
flies and bees
on the wallpaper,
it is like a warm fire, and
better than eating steak,
and the grass is green enough
and the sun is sun enough
and what's left of my life
stands there
checking glints of green flying;
it is a giant disrobing of
care, stumbling away from
doing.

suddenly I understand
old men in rockers
bats in Colorado caves
tiny lice crawling into
the eyes of dead birds.

back and forth
he follows his gasoline
sound. it is
interesting enough,
with
the streets
flat on their Spring backs
and smiling.

crucifix in a deathhand

yes, they begin out in a willow, I think
the starch mountains begin out in the willow
and keep right on going without regard for
pumas and nectarines
somehow these mountains are like
an old woman with a bad memory and
a shopping basket.
we are in a basin. that is the
idea. down in the sand and the alleys,
this land punched-in, cuffed-out, divided,
held like a crucifix in a deathhand,
this land bought, resold, bought again and
sold again, the wars long over,
the Spaniards all the way back in Spain
down in the thimble again, and now
real estaters, subdividers, landlords, freeway
engineers arguing. this is their land and
I walk on it, live on it a little while
near Hollywood here I see young men in rooms
listening to glazed recordings
and I think too of old men sick of music
sick of everything, and death like suicide
I think is sometimes voluntary, and to get your
hold on the land here it is best to return to the
Grand Central Market, see the old Mexican women,
the poor . . . I am sure you have seen these same women
many years before
arguing
with the same young Japanese clerks
witty, knowledgeable and golden
among their soaring store of oranges, apples

avocados, tomatoes, cucumbers —
and you know how *these* look, they do look good
as if you could eat them all
light a cigar and smoke away the bad world.
then it's best to go back to the bars, the same bars
wooden, stale, merciless, green
with the young policeman walking through
scared and looking for trouble,
and the beer is still bad
it has an edge that already mixes with vomit and
decay, and you've got to be strong in the shadows
to ignore it, to ignore the poor and to ignore yourself
and the shopping bag between your legs
down there feeling good with its avocados and
oranges and fresh fish and wine bottles, who needs
a Fort Lauderdale winter?
25 years ago there used to be a whore there
with a film over one eye, who was too fat
and made little silver bells out of cigarette
tinfoil. the sun seemed warmer then
although this was probably not
true, and you take your shopping bag
outside and walk along the street
and the green beer hangs there
just above your stomach like
a short and shameful shawl, and
you look around and no longer
see any
old men.

the screw-game

one of the terrible things is
really
being in bed
night after night
with a woman you no longer
want to screw.

they get old, they don't look very good
anymore—they even tend to
snore, lose
spirit.

so, in bed, you turn sometimes,
your foot touches hers—
god, *awful!*—
and the night is out there
beyond the curtains
sealing you together
in the
tomb.

and in the morning you go to the
bathroom, pass in the hall, talk,
say odd things; eggs fry, motors
start.

but sitting across
you have 2 strangers
jamming toast into mouths
burning the sullen head and gut with
coffee.

in 10 million places in America
it is the same—
stale lives propped against each
other
and no place to
go.

you get in the car
and you drive to work
and there are more strangers there, most of them
wives and husbands of somebody
else, and besides the guillotine of work, they
flirt and joke and pinch, sometimes tend to
work off a quick screw somewhere—
they can't do it at home—
and then
the drive back home
waiting for Christmas or Labor Day or
Sunday or
something.

millionaires

you
no faces
no faces
at all
laughing at nothing—
let me tell you
I have drunk in skid row rooms with
imbecile winos
whose cause was better
whose eyes still held some light
whose voices retained some sensibility,
and when the morning came
we were sick but not ill,
poor but not deluded,
and we stretched in our beds and rose
in the late afternoons
like millionaires.

**when you wait for the dawn to crawl through the
screen like a burglar to take your life away**

the snake had crawled the hole,
and she said,
tell me about
yourself.

and
I said,
I was beaten down
long ago
in some alley
in another
world.

and she said,
we're all
like pigs
slapped down some lane,
our
grassbrains
singing
toward the
blade.

by
god,
you're an
odd one,
I said.

we
sat there

smoking
cigarettes
at
5
in the morning.

the talkers

the boy walks with his muddy feet across my
soul
talking about recitals, virtuosi, conductors,
the lesser known novels of Dostoyevsky;
talking about how he corrected a waitress,
a hasher who didn't know that French dressing
was composed of *so and so;*
he gabbles about the Arts until
I hate the Arts,
and there is nothing cleaner
than getting back to a bar or
back to the track and watching them run,
watching things go without this
clamor and chatter,
talk, talk, talk,
the small mouth going, the eyes blinking,
a boy, a child, sick with the Arts,
grabbing at it like the skirt of a mother,
and I wonder how many tens of thousands
there are like him across the land
on rainy nights
on sunny mornings
on evenings meant for peace
in concert halls
in cafes
at poetry recitals
talking, soiling, arguing.

it's like a pig going to bed
with a good woman
and you don't want
the woman any more.

art

as the
spirit
wanes
the
form
appears.

advice for some young man in the year 2064 A.D.

let me speak as a friend
although the centuries hang
between us and neither you nor I
can see the moon.

be careful less the onion blind the eye
or the snake sting
or the beetle possess the house
or the lover your wife
or the government your child
or the wine your will
or the doctor your heart
or the butcher your belly
or the cat your chair
or the lawyer your ignorance of the law
or the law dressed as a uniformed man and killing you.

dismiss perfection as an ache of the
greedy
but do not give in to the mass modesty of
easy imperfection.

and remember
the belly of the whale is laden with
great men.

(uncollected)

ice for the eagles

I keep remembering the horses
under the moon
I keep remembering feeding the horses
sugar
white oblongs of sugar
more like ice,
and they had heads like
eagles
bald heads that could bite and
did not.

The horses were more real than
my father
more real than God
and they could have stepped on my
feet but they didn't
they could have done all kinds of horrors
but they didn't.

I was almost 5
but I have not forgotten yet;
o my god they were strong and good
those red tongues slobbering
out of their souls.

girl in a miniskirt reading the Bible outside my window

Sunday. I am eating a
grapefruit. church is over at the Russian
Orthodox to the
west.
she is dark
of Eastern descent,
large brown eyes look up from the Bible
then down. a small red and black
Bible, and as she reads
her legs keep moving, moving,
she is doing a slow rhythmic dance
reading the Bible . . .
long gold earrings;
2 gold bracelets on each arm,
and it's a mini-*suit*, I suppose,
the cloth hugs her body,
the lightest of tans is that cloth,
she twists this way and that,
long young legs warm in the sun . . .

there is no escaping her being
there is no desire to . . .
my radio is playing symphonic music
that she cannot hear
but her movements coincide *exactly*

to the rhythms of the
symphony . . .

she is dark, she is dark
she is reading about God.

I am God.

hell is a lonely place

he was 65, his wife was 66, had
Alzheimer's disease.

he had cancer of the
mouth.
there were
operations, radiation
treatments
which decayed the bones in his
jaw
which then had to be
wired.

daily he put his wife in
rubber diapers
like a
baby.

unable to drive in his
condition
he had to take a taxi to
the medical
center,
had difficulty speaking,
had to
write the directions
down.

on his last visit
they informed him
there would be another
operation: a bit more

left
cheek and a bit more
tongue.

when he returned
he changed his wife's
diapers
put on the tv
dinners, watched the
evening news
then went to the
bedroom, got the
gun, put it to her
temple, fired.

she fell to the
left, he sat upon the
couch
put the gun into his
mouth, pulled the
trigger.

the shots didn't arouse
the neighbors.

later
the burning tv dinners
did.

somebody arrived, pushed
the door open, saw
it.

soon
the police arrived and
went through their
routine, found
some items:
a closed savings
account and
a checkbook with a
balance of
$1.14

suicide, they
deduced.

in three weeks
there were two
new tenants:
a computer engineer
named
Ross
and his wife
Anatana
who studied
ballet.

they looked like another
upwardly mobile
pair.

the girls and the birds

the girls were young
and worked the
streets
but often couldn't
score, they
ended up
in my hotel
room
3 or 4 of
them
sucking at the
wine,
hair in face,
runs in
stockings,
cursing, telling
stories . . .

somehow
those were
peaceful
nights

but really
they reminded me
of long
ago
when I was a
boy
watching my grand-
mother's
canaries make

droppings
into their
seed
and into their
water
and the
canaries were
beautiful
and
chattered
but
never
sang.

1813–1883

listening to Wagner
as outside in the dark the wind blows a cold rain the
trees wave and shake lights go
off and on the walls creak and the cats run under the
bed . . .

Wagner battles the agonies, he's emotional but
solid, he's the supreme fighter, a giant in a world of
pygmies, he takes it straight on through, he breaks
barriers
an
astonishing FORCE of sound as

everything here shakes
shivers
bends
blasts
in fierce gamble

yes, Wagner and the storm intermix with the wine as
nights like this run up my wrists and up into my head and
back down into the
gut

some men never
die
and some men never
live

but we're all alive
tonight.

no leaders, please

invent yourself and then reinvent yourself,
don't swim in the same slough.
invent yourself and then reinvent yourself
and
stay out of the clutches of mediocrity.

invent yourself and then reinvent yourself,
change your tone and shape so often that they can
never
categorize you.

reinvigorate yourself and
accept what is
but only on the terms that you have invented
and reinvented.

be self-taught.

and reinvent your life because you must;
it is your life and
its history
and the present
belong only to
you.

song

Julio came by with his guitar and sang his
latest song.
Julio was famous, he wrote songs and also
published books of little drawings and
poems.
they were very
good.

Julio sang a song about his latest love
affair.
he sang that
it began so well
then it went to
hell.

those were not the words exactly
but that was the meaning of the
words.

Julio finished
singing.

then he said, "I still care for
her, I can't get her off my
mind."

"what will I do?" Julio
asked.

"drink," Henry said,
pouring.

Julio just looked at his
glass:
"I wonder what she's doing
now?"

"probably engaging in oral
copulation," Henry
suggested.

Julio put his guitar back in
the case and
walked to the
door.

Henry walked Julio to his car which
was parked in the
drive.

it was a nice moonlit
night.

as Julio started his car and
backed out the drive
Henry waved him a
farewell.

then he went inside
sat
down.

he finished Julio's untouched
drink

then he
phoned
her.

"he was just by," Henry told
her, "he's feeling very
bad . . ."

"you'll have to excuse me,"
she said, "but I'm busy right
now."

she hung
up.

and Henry poured one of his
own
as outside the crickets sang
their own
song.

one for Sherwood Anderson

sometimes I forget about him and his peculiar
innocence, almost idiotic, awkward and mawkish,
he liked walking over bridges and through cornfields.
tonight I think about him, the way the lines were,
one felt space between his lines, air
and he told it so the lines remained
carved there
something like van Gogh.
he took his time
looking about
sometimes running to save something
leaving everything to save something,
then at other times giving it all away.
he didn't understand Hemingway's neon tattoo,
found Faulkner much too clever.
he was a midwestern hick
he took his time.
he was as far away from Fitzgerald as he was
from Paris.
he told stories and left the meaning open
and sometimes he told meaningless stories
because that was the way it was.
he told the same story again and again
and he never wrote a story that was unreadable.
and nobody ever talks about his life or
his death.

bow wow love

here things are tough but
they're mostly always tough.
basically I'm just trying to get along
with the female. when you
first meet them their eyes
are all moist with under-
standing; laughter abounds
like sand fleas. then, Je-
sus, time tinkles on and
things leak. they
start BOOMING out DEMANDS.
and, actually, what they
demand is basically contrary to what-
ever you are or could be.
what's so strange is the sudden
knowledge that they've never
read anything you've writ-
ten, not really read it at
all. or worse, if they have,
they've come to SAVE
you! which means mainly
wanting you to act like everybody
else and be just like them
and their friends. mean-
while they've sucked
you up and wound you up
in a million webs, and
being somewhat of a
feeling person you *can't*
help but remember their
good side or the side
that at first *seemed* to be good.

and so you find yourself
alone in your
bedroom grabbing your
gut and saying, o, shit
no, not again.

we should have known.
maybe we wanted cotton
candy luck. maybe we
believed. what trash.
we believed like dogs
believe.

(uncollected)

the day the epileptic spoke

the other day
I'm out at the track
betting Early Bird
(that's when you bet at the
track before it opens)
I am sitting there having
a coffee and going over
the Form
and this guy slides toward
me—
his body is twisted
his head shakes
his eyes are out of
focus
there is spittle upon his
lips

he manages to get close to
me and asks,
"pardon me, sir, but could you
tell me the number of
Lady of Dawn in the
first race?"

"it's the 7 horse,"
I tell him.

"thank you, sir,"
he says.

that night
or the next morning

really:
12:04 a.m.
Los Alamitos Quarter Horse
Results on radio
KLAC
the man told me
Lady of Dawn
won the first at
$79.80

that was two weeks
ago
and I've been there
every racing day since
and I haven't seen that
poor epileptic fellow
again.

the gods have ways of
telling you things
when you think you know
a lot

or worse—

when you think
you know
just a
little.

when Hugo Wolf went mad—

Hugo Wolf went mad while eating an onion
and writing his 253rd song; it was rainy
April and the worms came out of the ground
humming *Tannhäuser*, and he spilled his milk
with his ink, and his blood fell out to the walls
and he howled and he roared and he screamed, and
down-
stairs his landlady said, I *knew* it, that rotten son
of a
bitch has dummied up his brain, he's jacked-off
his last piece
of music and now I'll never get the rent, and some-
day he'll be fam-
ous and they'll bury him in the rain, but right now
I wish he'd shut
up that god damned screaming—for my money he's
a silly pansy jackass
and when they move him out of here, I hope they
move in a good solid fish-
erman
or a hangman
or a seller of
biblical tracts.

in a neighborhood of
murder

the roaches spit out
paper clips
and the helicopter circles and circles
smelling for blood
searchlights leering down into our
bedroom

5 guys in this court have pistols
another a
machete
we are all murderers and
alcoholics
but there are worse in the hotel
across the street
they sit in the green and white doorway
banal and depraved
waiting to be institutionalized

here we each have a small green plant
in the window
and when we fight with our women at 3 a.m.
we speak
softly
and on each porch
is a small dish of food
always eaten by morning
we presume
by the
cats.

**the strangest sight you ever did
see—**

I had this room in front on DeLongpre
and I used to sit for hours
in the daytime
looking out the front
window.
there were any number of girls who would
walk by
swaying;
it helped my afternoons,
added something to the beer and the
cigarettes.

one day I saw something
extra.
I heard the sound of it first.
"come on, push!" he said.
there was a long board
about 2½ feet wide and
8 feet long;
nailed to the ends and in the middle
were roller skates.
he was pulling in front
two long ropes attached to the board
and she was in back
guiding and also pushing.
all their possessions were tied to the
board:
pots, pans, bed quilts, and so forth
were roped to the board
tied down;
and the skate wheels were grinding.

he was white, red-necked, a
southerner—
thin, slumped, his pants about to
fall from his
ass—
his face pinked by the sun and
cheap wine,
and she was black
and walked upright
pushing;
she was simply beautiful
in turban
long green earrings
yellow dress
from
neck to
ankle.
her face was gloriously
indifferent.

"don't worry!" he shouted, looking back
at her, "somebody will
rent us a place!"

she didn't answer.

then they were gone
although I still heard the
skate wheels.

they're going to make it,
I thought.

I'm sure they
did.

the 2nd novel

they'd come around and
they'd ask
"you finished your
2nd novel yet?"

"no."

"whatsamatta? whatsamatta
that you can't
finish it?"

"hemorrhoids and
insomnia."

"maybe you've lost
it?"

"lost what?"

"you know."

now when they come
around I tell them,
"yeh. I finished
it. be out in Sept."

"you *finished* it?"

"yeh."

"well, listen, I gotta
go."

even the cat
here in the courtyard
won't come to my door
anymore.

it's nice.

junk

sitting in a dark bedroom with 3 junkies,
female.
brown paper bags filled with trash are
everywhere.
it is one-thirty in the afternoon.
they talk about madhouses,
hospitals.
they are waiting for a fix.
none of them work.
it's relief and food stamps and
Medi-Cal.

men are usable objects
toward the fix.

it is one-thirty in the afternoon
and outside small plants grow.
their children are still in school.
the females smoke cigarettes
and suck listlessly on beer and
tequila
which I have purchased.

I sit with them.
I wait on my fix:
I am a poetry junkie.

they pulled Ezra through the streets
in a wooden cage.
Blake was sure of God.
Villon was a mugger.

Lorca sucked cock.
T. S. Eliot worked a teller's cage.

most poets are swans,
egrets.

I sit with 3 junkies
at one-thirty in the afternoon.

the smoke pisses upward.

I wait.

death is a nothing jumbo.

one of the females says that she likes
my yellow shirt.

I believe in a simple violence.

this is
some of it.

Mademoiselle from Armentières

if you gotta have wars
I suppose World War One was the best.
really, you know, both sides were much more enthusiastic,
they really had something to fight for,
they really thought they had something to fight for,
it was bloody and wrong but it was Romantic,
those dirty Germans with babies stuck on the ends of their
bayonets, and so forth, and
there were lots of patriotic songs, and the women loved *both* the
    soldiers
and their money.

the Mexican war and those other wars hardly ever happened.
and the Civil War, that was just a movie.

the wars come too fast now
even the pro-war boys grow weary,
World War Two did them in,
and then Korea, that Korea,
that was dirty, nobody won
except the black marketeers,
and BAM! — then came Vietnam,
I suppose the historians will have a name and a meaning for it,
but the young wised up first
and now the old are getting wise,
almost everybody's anti-war,
no use having a war you can't win,
right or wrong.

hell, I remember when I was a kid it
was 10 or 15 years after World War One was over,
we built model planes of Spads and Fokkers,

we bought *Flying Aces* magazine at the newsstand
we knew about Baron Manfred von Richthofen
and Capt. Eddie Rickenbacker
and we fought in dream trenches with our dream rifles
and had dream
bayonet fights with the dirty
Hun . . .
and those movies, full of drama and excitement,
about good old World War One, where
we almost got the Kaiser, we almost kidnapped him
once,
and in the end
we finished off all those spike-helmeted bastards
forever.

the young kids now, they don't build model warplanes
nor do they dream fight in dream rice paddies,
they know it's all useless, ordinary,
just a job like
sweeping the streets or picking up the garbage,
they'd rather go watch a Western or hang out at the
mall or go to the zoo or a football game, they're
already thinking of college and automobiles and wives
and homes and barbecues, they're already trapped
in another kind of dream, another kind of war,
and I guess it won't kill them as fast, at least not
physically.

it was wrong but World War One was fun for us
it gave us Jean Harlow and James Cagney
and "Mademoiselle from Armentières, Parley-Voo?"
it gave us

long afternoons and evenings of play
(we didn't realize that many of us were soon to die in
    another war)
yes, they fooled us nicely but we were young and loved it—
the lies of our elders—
and see how it has changed—
they can't bullshit
even a kid anymore,
not about all that.

now

I had boils the size of tomatoes
all over me
they stuck a drill into me
down at the county hospital,
and
just as the sun went down
every day
there was a man in a nearby ward
he'd start hollering for his friend Joe.
JOE! he'd holler, OH JOE! JOE! J O E!
COME GET ME, JOE!

Joe never came by.
I've never heard such mournful
sounds.

Joe was probably working off a
piece of ass or
attempting to solve a crossword puzzle.

I've always said
if you want to find out who your friends are
go to a madhouse or
jail.

and if you want to find out where love is not
be a perpetual
loser.

I was very lucky with my boils
being drilled and tortured
against the backdrop of the Sierra Madre mountains

while that sun went down;
when that sun went down I knew what *I* would do
when I finally got that drill in my hands
like I have it
now.

society should realize . . .

you consult psychiatrists and philosophers
when things aren't going well
and whores when they are.
the whores are there for young boys and old
men; to the young boys they say,
"don't be frightened, honey, here I'll put it
in for you."
and for the old guys
they put on an act
like you're really hooking it home.
society should realize the value of the
whore—I mean, those girls who really enjoy their
work—those who make it almost an
art form.

I'm thinking of the time
in a Mexican whorehouse
this gal with her little bowl and her rag
washing my dick,
and it got hard and she laughed and I
laughed and she
kissed it, gently and slowly, then she walked over and
spread out
on the bed
and I got on and we worked easily, no effort, no
tension, and some guy beat on the door and
yelled,
"Hey! what the hell's going on in there?
Hurry it up!"
but it was like a Mahler symphony—you just don't
rush
it.

when I finished and she came back, there was
the bowl and the rag again
and we both laughed; then she kissed it
gently and
slowly, and I got up and put my clothes back on and
walked out—
"Jesus, buddy, what the hell were ya doin' in
there?"
"Fuckin'," I told the gentleman
and walked down the hall and down the steps and stood
outside in the road and lit one of those
sweet Mexican cigarettes in the moonlight.
liberated and human again
for a mere $3, I
loved the night, Mexico and
myself.

the souls of dead animals

after the slaughterhouse
there was a bar around the corner
and I sat in there
and watched the sun go down
through the window,
a window that overlooked a lot
full of tall dry weeds.

I never showered with the boys at the
plant
after work
so I smelled of sweat and
blood.
the smell of sweat lessens after a
while
but the blood-smell begins to fulminate
and gain power.

I smoked cigarettes and drank beer
until I felt good enough to
board the bus
with the souls of all those dead
animals riding with
me;
heads would turn slightly
women would rise and move away from
me.

when I got off the bus
I only had a block to walk
and one stairway up to my

room
where I'd turn on my radio and
light a cigarette
and nobody minded me
at all.

the tragedy of the leaves

I awakened to dryness and the ferns were dead,
the potted plants yellow as corn;
my woman was gone
and the empty bottles like bled corpses
surrounded me with their uselessness;
the sun was still good, though,
and my landlady's note cracked in fine and
undemanding yellowness; what was needed now
was a good comedian, ancient style, a jester
with jokes upon absurd pain; pain is absurd
because it exists, nothing more;
I shaved carefully with an old razor
the man who had once been young and
said to have genius; but
that's the tragedy of the leaves,
the dead ferns, the dead plants;
and I walked into a dark hall
where the landlady stood
execrating and final,
sending me to hell,
waving her fat, sweaty arms
and screaming
screaming for rent
because the world had failed us
both.

the birds

the acute and terrible air hangs with murder
as summer birds mingle in the branches
and warble
and mystify the clamor of the mind;
an old parrot
who never talks,
sits thinking in a Chinese laundry,
disgruntled
forsaken
celibate;
there is red on his wing
where there should be green,
and between us
the recognition of
an immense and wasted life.

. . . my 2nd wife left me
because I set our birds free:
one yellow, with crippled wing
quickly going down and to the left,
cat-meat,
cackling like an organ;
and the other,
mean green,
of empty thimble head,
popping up like a rocket
high into the hollow sky,
disappearing like sour love
and yesterday's desire
and leaving me
forever.

and when my wife
returned that night
with her bags and plans,
her tricks and shining greeds,
she found me
glittering over a yellow feather
seeking out the music
which she,
oddly,
failed to
hear.

the loner

16 and one-half inch
neck
68 years old
lifts weights
body like a young
boy (almost)

kept his head
shaved
and drank port wine
from half-gallon jugs

kept the chain on the
door
windows boarded

you had to give
a special knock
to get in

he had brass knucks
knives
clubs
guns

he had a chest like a
wrestler
never lost his
glasses

never swore
never looked for
trouble

never married after the death
of his only
wife

hated
cats
roaches
mice
humans

worked crossword
puzzles
kept up with the
news

that 16 and one-half inch
neck

for 68 he was
something

all those boards
across the windows

washed his own underwear
and socks

my friend Red took me up
to meet him
one night

we talked a while
together

then we left

Red asked, "what do you
think?"

I answered, "more afraid to die
than the rest of us."

I haven't seen either of them
since.

The Genius of the Crowd

There is enough treachery, hatred,
                        violence,
Absurdity in the average human
                    being
To supply any given army on any given
   day.
AND The Best At Murder Are Those
    Who Preach Against It.
AND The Best At Hate Are Those
    Who Preach LOVE
AND THE BEST AT WAR
    —FINALLY—ARE THOSE WHO
PREACH
                        PEACE

Those Who Preach GOD
    NEED God
Those Who Preach PEACE
    Do Not Have Peace.
THOSE WHO PREACH LOVE
    DO NOT HAVE LOVE
BEWARE THE PREACHERS
Beware The Knowers.

      Beware
      Those Who
      Are ALWAYS
      READING
      BOOKS

Beware Those Who Either Detest
    Poverty Or Are Proud Of It

BEWARE Those Quick To Praise
For They Need PRAISE In Return

BEWARE Those Quick To Censure:
They Are Afraid Of What They Do
Not Know

Beware Those Who Seek Constant
Crowds; They Are Nothing
Alone

     Beware
     The Average Man
     The Average Woman
     BEWARE Their Love

Their Love Is Average, Seeks
Average
But There Is Genius In Their Hatred
There Is Enough Genius In Their
Hatred To Kill You, To Kill
Anybody.

Not Wanting Solitude
Not Understanding Solitude
They Will Attempt To Destroy
Anything
That Differs
From Their Own

     Not Being Able
     To Create Art

They Will Not
Understand Art

They Will Consider Their Failure
As Creators
Only As A Failure
Of The World

Not Being Able To Love Fully
They Will BELIEVE Your Love
Incomplete
AND THEN THEY WILL HATE
YOU

And Their Hatred Will Be Perfect
Like A Shining Diamond
Like A Knife
Like A Mountain
LIKE A TIGER
LIKE Hemlock

Their Finest
ART

German bar

I had lost the last race big
somebody had stolen my coat
I could feel the flu coming on
and my tires were
low. I went in to get a
beer at the German bar
but the waitress was having a fit
her heart strangled by disappointment
grief and loss.
women get troubled all at once,
you know. I left a tip
and got out.

nobody wins.
ask Caesar.

the snow of Italy

over my radio now
comes the sound of a truly mad organ,
I can see some monk
drunk in a cellar
mind gone or found,
talking to God in a different way;
I see candles and this man has a red beard
as God has a red beard;
it is snowing, it is Italy, it is cold
and the bread is hard
and there is no butter,
only wine
wine in purple bottles
with giraffe necks,
and now the organ rises, again,
he violates it,
he plays it like a madman,
there is blood and spit in his beard,
he wants to laugh but there isn't time,
the sun is going out,
then his fingers slow,
now there is exhaustion and the dream,
yes, even holiness,
man going to man,
to the mountain, the elephant, the star,
and a candle falls
but continues to burn upon its side,
a wax puddle shining in the eyes
of my red monk,
there is moss on the walls
and the stain of thought and failure and
waiting,

then again the music comes like hungry tigers,
and he laughs,
it is a child's laugh, an idiot's laugh,
laughing at nothing,
the only laugh that understands,
he holds the keys down
like stopping everything
and the room blooms with madness,
and then he stops, stops,
and sits, the candles burning,
one up, one down,
the snow of Italy is all that's left,
it is over: the essence and the pattern.
I watch as
he pinches out the candles with his fingers,
wincing near the outer edge of each eye
and the room is dark
as everything has always been.

**for Jane: with all the love I had,
which was not enough:**

I pick up the skirt,
I pick up the sparkling beads
in black,
this thing that moved once
around flesh,
and I call God a liar,
I say anything that moved
like that
or knew
my name
could never die
in the common verity of dying,
and I pick
up her lovely
dress,
all her loveliness gone,
and I speak
to all the gods,
Jewish gods, Christ-gods,
chips of blinking things,
idols, pills, bread,
fathoms, risks,
knowledgeable surrender,
rats in the gravy of 2 gone quite mad
without a chance,
hummingbird knowledge, hummingbird chance,
I lean upon this,
I lean on all of this

and I know:
her dress upon my arm:
but
they will not
give her back to me.

notice

the swans drown in bilge water,
take down the signs,
test the poisons,
barricade the cow
from the bull,
the peony from the sun,
take the lavender kisses from my night,
put the symphonies out on the streets
like beggars,
get the nails ready,
flog the backs of the saints,
stun frogs and mice for the cat,
burn the enthralling paintings,
piss on the dawn,
my love
is dead.

for Jane

225 days under grass
and you know more than I.

they have long taken your blood,
you are a dry stick in a basket.

is this how it works?

in this room
the hours of love
still make shadows.

when you left
you took almost
everything.

I kneel in the nights
before tigers
that will not let me be.

what you were
will not happen again.

the tigers have found me
and I do not care.

eulogy to a hell of a
dame

some dogs who sleep at night
must dream of bones
and I remember your bones
in flesh
and best
in that dark green dress
and those high-heeled bright
black shoes,
you always cursed when you
drank,
your hair coming down you
wanted to explode out of
what was holding you:
rotten memories of a
rotten
past, and
you finally got
out
by dying,
leaving me with the
rotten
present;
you've been dead
28 years
yet I remember you
better than any of
the rest;
you were the only one
who understood
the futility of the
arrangement of

life;
all the others were only
displeased with
trivial segments,
carped
nonsensically about
nonsense;
Jane, you were
killed by
knowing too much.
here's a drink
to your bones
that
this dog
still
dreams about.

barfly

Jane, who has been dead for 31 years,
never could have
imagined that I would write a screenplay of our drinking
days together
and
that it would be made into a movie
and
that a beautiful movie star would play her
part.

I can hear Jane now: "A beautiful movie star? oh,
for Christ's sake!"

Jane, that's show biz, so go back to sleep, dear, because
no matter how hard they tried they
just *couldn't* find anybody exactly like
you.

and neither can
I.

was Li Po wrong?

you know what Li Po said when asked if he'd rather be an
Artist or Rich?
"I'd rather be Rich," he replied, "for Artists can usually be found
sitting on the doorsteps of the
Rich."
I've sat on the doorsteps of some expensive and
unbelievable homes
myself
but somehow I always managed to disgrace myself and / or insult
my Rich hosts
(mostly after drinking large quantities of their fine
liquor).
perhaps I was afraid of the Rich?
all I knew then was poverty and the very poor,
and I felt instinctively that the Rich shouldn't be so
Rich,
that it was some kind of clever
twist of fate
based on something rotten and
unfair.
of course, one could say the same thing
about being poor,
only there were so many poor, it all seemed completely
out of proportion.
and so when I, as an Artist, visited the
homes of the Rich, I felt ashamed to be
there, and I drank too much of their fine wines,
broke their expensive glassware and antique dishes,
burned cigarette holes in their Persian rugs and
mauled their wives,
reacting badly to the whole damned
situation.

yet I had no political or social solution.
I was just a lousy houseguest,
I guess,
and after a while
I protected both myself and the Rich
by rejecting their
invitations
and everybody felt much better after
that.
I went back to
drinking alone,
breaking my own cheap glassware,
filling the room with cigar
smoke and feeling
wonderful
instead of feeling trapped,
used,
pissed on,
fucked.

the night I saw George Raft in Vegas

I bet on #6, I try red, I stare at the women's legs and breasts,
I wonder what Chekhov would do, and over in the corner three
    men with
blue plates sit eating the carnage of my youth, they have beards
and look very much like Russians and I pat an imaginary pistol
    over
my left tit and try to smile like George Raft sizing up a French
    tart. I play
the field, I pull out dollars like turnips from the good earth, the
    lights
blaze and nobody says stop.

Hank, says my whore, for Christ's sake you're losing everything
    except me,
and I say don't forget, baby, I'm a shipping clerk. what've I got
    to lose
but a ball of string?

the gentlemen in the corner who look like Russians get up, knock
their plates and cups on the floor and wipe their mouths on the
    tablecloth.
some belch (and one farts). they laugh evilly and leave without
    anyone bother-
ing them. a ribbed and moiled cat comes out of somewhere,
begins licking the plates on the floor and then jumps up on the
table and walks around like his feet are wet.

I try black. the croupier's eyes dart like beetles. he makes futile
almost habitual movements to brush them away.

I switch back to red. I look around for George Raft and spill my
    drink

against my chest. Hank, says my whore, let's get out of here!
    well, at least,
I say, I ought to get a blow job out of this. you needn't get filthy,
    the whore
says. I say, baby, I was born filthy. I try #14.

DEATH COMES SLOWLY LIKE ANTS TO A FALLEN FIG.

mirrors enclose us, I say to the croupier, ignoring the scenery of
    our despair.

I slap away a filthy thing that runs across my mouth. the cat
leaps and snatches it up as it spins upon its back kicking its
thousand legs.

then George Raft walks in. hello kid, he says, back again? I place
my last few coins on the chest of a dead elephant.
the lightning flares, they are stabbing grapefruit in the backroom,
    some-
body drops a glove and the place, the whole place, goes up in
    smoke.

we walk back to the car and fall asleep.

I am eaten by butterflies

maybe I'll win the Irish Sweepstakes
maybe I'll go nuts
maybe Harcourt Brace will call
or maybe unemployment insurance or
a rich lesbian at the top of a hill.

maybe reincarnation as a frog . . .
or $70,000 found floating in a plastic sack
in the bathtub.

I need help
I am a thin man being eaten by
green trees
butterflies and
you.

turn turn
light the lamp
my teeth ache the teeth of my soul ache
I can't sleep I
pray for the dead
the white mice
engines on fire
blood on a green gown in an operating room
and I am caught
ow ow
wild: my body being there filled with nothing but
me
me caught halfway between suicide and
old age
hustling in factories next to the
young boys

keeping pace
burning my blood like gasoline and
making the foreman
grin.

my poems are only bits of scratchings
on the floor of a
cage.

(uncollected)

the veryest

here comes the fishhead singing
here comes the baked potato in drag
here comes nothing to do all day long
here comes another night of no sleep
here comes the phone ringing the wrong voice
here comes a termite with a banjo
here comes a flagpole with blank eyes
here comes a cat and a dog wearing nylons
here comes a machine gun singing
here comes bacon burning in the pan
here comes a voice saying something dull with authority
here comes a newspaper stuffed with small red birds
with flat brown beaks
here comes a woman carrying a torch
a grenade
a deathly love
here comes victory carrying one bucket of guts
and one bucket of blood
while stumbling over the berry bush
and here comes a little lamb
and here comes Mary at last
and the sheet hangs out the window
and the bombers head east west north south
get lost
get tossed like salad
all the fish in the sea line up and form
one line
one long line
one very long long line
the veryest longest line you could ever imagine
and we get lost
walking past purple mountains.

we walk lost
bare at last like the knife blade
or the electric shock
having given
having spit it out like an unexpected olive seed
as the girl at the call service
screams over the phone:
"don't call back! you sound like a jerk!"

(uncollected)

man mowing the lawn across the way from me

I watch you walking with your machine.
ah, you're too stupid to be cut like grass,
you're too stupid to let anything violate you—
the girls won't use their knives on you
they don't want to
their sharp edge is wasted on you,
you are interested only in baseball games and
western movies and grass blades.

can't you take just one of my knives?
here's an old one—stuck into me in 1955,
she's dead now, it wouldn't hurt much.
I can't give you this last one—
I can't pull it out yet,
but here's one from 1964, how about taking
this 1964 one from me?

man mowing the lawn across the way from me
don't you have a knife somewhere in your gut
where love left?

man mowing the lawn across the way from me
don't you have a knife somewhere deep in your heart
where love left?

man mowing the lawn across the way from me
don't you see the young girls walking down the sidewalks now
with knives in their purses?
don't you see their beautiful eyes and dresses and
hair?
don't you see their beautiful asses and knees and
ankles?

man mowing the lawn across the way from me
is that all you see—those grass blades?
is that all you hear—the drone of the mower?

I can see all the way to Italy
                    to Japan
                    to the Honduras
I can see the young girls sharpening their knives
in the morning and at noon and at night, and
especially at night, o,
especially at night.

oh, yes

there are worse things than
being alone
but it often takes decades
to realize this
and most often
when you do
it's too late
and there's nothing worse
than
too late.

poop

I remember, he told me, that when I was 6 or
7 years old my mother was always taking me
to the doctor and saying, "he hasn't pooped."

she was always asking me, "have you
pooped?"
it seemed to be her favorite question.
and, of course, I couldn't lie, I had real problems
pooping.
I was all knotted up inside.
my parents did that to me.

I looked at those huge beings, my father,
my mother, and they seemed really stupid.
sometimes I thought they were just pretending
to be stupid because nobody could really be that
stupid.
but they weren't pretending.
they had me all knotted up inside like a pretzel.

I mean, I *had* to live with them, they told
me what to do and how to do it and when.
they fed, housed and clothed me.
and worst of all, there was no other place for
me to go, no other choice:
I had to stay with them.

I mean, I didn't know much at that age
but I could sense that they were lumps
of flesh and little else.

dinnertime was the worst, a nightmare
of slurps, spittle and idiotic conversation.
I looked straight down at my plate and tried
to swallow my food but
it all turned to glue inside.
I couldn't digest my parents or the food.

that must have been it, for it was hell for me
to poop.

"have you pooped?"
and there I'd be in the doctor's office once again.
he had a little more sense than my parents but
not much.

"well, well, my little man, so you haven't pooped?"

he was fat with bad breath and body odor and
had a pocket watch with a large gold chain
that dangled across his gut.

I thought, I bet he poops a load.

and I looked at my mother.
she had large buttocks,
I could picture her on the toilet,
sitting there a little cross-eyed, pooping.
she was so placid, so
like a pigeon.

poopers both, I knew it in my heart.
disgusting people.

"well, little man, you just can't poop,
huh?"

he made a little joke of it: he could,
she could, the world could.
I couldn't.

"well, now, we're going to give you
these pills.
and if they don't work, then guess
what?"

I didn't answer.

"come on, little man, tell me."

all right, I decided to say it.
I wanted to get out of there:

"an enema."

"an enema," he smiled.

then he turned to my mother.
"and are you all right, dear?"

"oh, I'm fine, doctor!"

sure she was.
she pooped whenever she wanted.

then we would leave the office.

"isn't the doctor a nice man?"

no answer from me.

"isn't he?"

"yes."

but in my mind I changed it to, yes,
he can poop.

he looked like a poop.
the whole world pooped while I
was knotted up inside like a pretzel.

then we would walk out on the street
and I would look at the people passing
and all the people had behinds.

"that's all I ever noticed," he told me,
"it was horrible."

"we must have had similar
childhoods," I said.

"somehow, that doesn't help at all,"
he said.

"we've both got to get over this
thing," I said.

"I'm trying," he
answered.

Phillipe's 1950

Phillipe's is an old time
cafe off Alameda street
just a little north and east of
the main post office.
Phillipe's opens at 5 a.m.
and serves a cup of coffee
with cream and sugar
for a nickel.

in the early mornings
the bums come down off Bunker Hill,
as they say,
"with our butts wrapped
around our ears."
Los Angeles nights have a way
of getting very
cold.
"Phillipe's," they say,
"is the only place that doesn't
hassle us."

the waitresses are old
and most of the bums are
too.

come down there some
early morning.

for a nickel
you can see the most beautiful faces
in town.

downtown

nobody goes downtown anymore
the plants and trees have been cut away around
Pershing Square
the grass is brown
and the street preachers are not as good
as they used to be
and down on Broadway
the Latinos stand in long colorful lines
waiting to see Latino action movies.
I walk down to Clifton's cafeteria
it's still there
the waterfall is still there
the few white faces are old and poor
dignified
dressed in 1950s clothing
sitting at small tables on the first
floor.
I take my food upstairs to the
third floor—
all Latinos at the tables there
faces more tired than hostile
the men at rest from their factory jobs
their once beautiful wives now
heavy and satisfied
the men wanting badly to go out and raise hell
but now the money is needed for
clothing, tires, toys, TV sets
children's shoes, the rent.

I finish eating
walk down to the first floor and out,
and nearby is a penny arcade.

I remember it from the 1940s.
I walk in.
it is full of young Latinos and Blacks
between the ages of six and
fifteen
and they shoot machine guns
play mechanical soccer
and the piped-in salsa music is very
loud.
they fly spacecraft
test their strength
fight in the ring
have horse races
auto races
but none of them want their fortunes told.
I lean against a wall and
watch them.

I go outside again.
I walk down and across from the *Herald-
  Examiner* building
where my car is parked.
I get in. then I drive away.
it's Sunday. and it's true
like they say: the old gang never
goes downtown anymore.

elephants in the zoo

in the afternoon
they lean against
one another
and you can see how much
they like the sun.

(uncollected)

girl on the escalator

as I go to the escalator
a young fellow and a lovely young girl
are ahead of me.
her pants, her blouse are skin-
tight.
as we ascend
she rests one foot on the
step above and her behind
assumes a fascinating shape.
the young man looks all
around.
he appears worried.
he looks at me.
I look
away.

no, young man, I am not looking,
I am *not* looking at your girl's behind.
don't worry, I respect her and I respect you.
in fact, I respect everything: the flowers that grow, young women,
children, all the animals, our precious complicated
universe, everyone and everything.

I sense that the young man now feels
better and I am glad for
him. I know his problem: the girl has
a mother, a father, maybe a sister or
brother, and undoubtedly a bunch of
unfriendly relatives and she likes to
dance and flirt and she likes to
go to the movies and sometimes she talks
and chews gum at the same time and

she enjoys really dumb TV shows and
she thinks she's a budding actress and she
doesn't always look so good and she has a
terrible temper and sometimes she almost goes
crazy and she can talk for hours on the
telephone and she wants to go to
Europe some summer soon and she wants you to
buy her a near-new Mercedes and she's in love with
Mel Gibson and her mother is a
drunk and her father is a racist
and sometimes when she drinks too much she
snores and she's often cold in bed and
she has a guru, a guy who met Christ
in the desert in 1978, and she wants to
be a dancer and she's unemployed and she
gets migraine headaches every time she
eats sugar or cheese.

I watch him take her
up
the escalator, his arm
protectively about her
waist, thinking he's
lucky,
thinking he's a real special
guy, thinking that
nobody in the world has
what he has.

and he's right, terribly
terribly right, his arm around
that warm bucket of

intestine,
bladder,
kidneys,
lungs,
salt,
sulphur,
carbon dioxide
and
phlegm.

lotsa
luck.

the shit shits

yes, it's dark in here.
can't open the door.
can't open the jam lid.
can't find a pair of socks that match.
I was born in Andernach in 1920 and never thought it
would be like this.

at the races today I was standing in the 5-win line.
this big fat guy with body odor
kept jamming his binoculars into my ass and I turned and
said,
"pardon me, sir. could you please stop jamming those goddamned
binocs into my ass?"
he just looked at me with little pig eyes—
rather pink with olive pits for pupils—
and the eyes just kept looking at me until I stepped away and then
got sick, vomited into a
trash can.

I keep getting letters from an uncle in Andernach who must be
95 years old and he keeps asking,
"my boy, why don't you WRITE?"
what can I write him? unfortunately
there is nothing that I can write.

I pull on my shorts and they rip.
sleep is impossible, I mean good sleep. I just get
small spurts of it, and then back to the job where the foreman
comes by:
"Chinaski, for a pieceworker you crawl like a snail!"

I'm sick and I'm tired and I don't know where to go or what to do.
well, at lunchtime we all ride down the elevator together
making jokes and laughing
and then we sit in the employees' cafeteria making jokes and
laughing and eating the recooked food;
first they buy it then they fry it
then they reheat it then they sell it, can't be a germ left in there
or a vitamin either.

but we joke and laugh
otherwise we would start
screaming.

on Saturday and Sunday when I don't have money to go to the track
I just lay in bed.
I never get out of bed.
I don't want to go to a movie;
it is shameful for a full-grown man to go to a movie alone.
and women are less than nothing. they terrify
me.

I wonder what Andernach is like?

I think that if they would let me just stay in bed I could
get well or strong or at least feel better;
but it's always up and back to the machine,
searching for stockings that match,
shorts that won't tear,
looking at my face in the mirror, disgusted with
my face.

my uncle, what is he thinking with his crazy
letters?

we are all little forgotten pieces of shit
only we walk and talk
laugh
make jokes
and
the shit shits.

some day I will tell that foreman off.
I will tell everybody off.
and walk down to the end of the road and
make swans out of the blackbirds and
lions out of berry leaves.

(uncollected)

203

big time loser

I was on the train to Del Mar and I left my seat
to go to the bar car. I had a beer and came
back and sat down.
"pardon me," said the lady next to me, "but you're
sitting in my husband's seat."
"oh yeah?" I said. I picked up my Racing Form
and began studying it. the first race looked tough.
then a man was standing there. "hey, buddy,
you're in my seat!"
"I already told him," said the lady, "but he didn't pay
any attention."
"This is *my* seat!" I told the man.
"it's bad enough he takes my seat," said the man
    looking
around, "but now he's reading my Racing Form!"
I looked up at him, he was puffing his chest out.
"look at you," I said, "puffing your goddamned
chest out!"
"you're in my seat, buddy!" he told me.
"look," I said, "I've been in this seat since the
train left the station. ask anybody!"
"no, that's not right," said a man behind me,
"*he* had that seat when the train left the
station!"
"are you sure?"
"sure I'm sure!"

I got up and walked to the next train car.
there was my empty seat by the window and there was
my Racing Form.

I went back to the other car. the
man was reading his Racing Form.
"hey," I started to say . . .
"forget it," said the man.
"just leave us alone," said his wife.

I walked back to my car, sat down and
looked out the window
pretending to be interested in the land-
scape,
happy that the people in my car didn't know what
the people in the other car knew.

commerce

I used to drive those trucks so hard
and for so long that
my right foot would
go dead from pushing down on the
accelerator.
delivery after delivery,
14 hours at a time
for $1.10 per hour
under the table,
up one-way alleys in the worst parts of
town.
at midnight or at high noon,
racing between tall buildings
always with the stink of something
dying or about to die
in the freight elevator
at your destination,
a self-operated elevator,
opening into a large bright room,
uncomfortably so
under unshielded lights
over the heads of many women
each bent mute over a machine,
crucified alive
on piecework,
to hand the package then
to a fat son of a bitch in red
suspenders.
he signs, ripping through the cheap
paper
with his ballpoint pen,

that's power,
that's America at work.

you think of killing him
on the spot
but discard that thought and
leave,
down into the urine-stinking
elevator,
they have you crucified too,
America at work,
where they rip out your intestines
and your brain and your
will and your spirit.
they suck you dry, then throw
you away.
the capitalist system.
the work ethic.
the profit motive.
the memory of your father's words,
"work hard and you'll be
appreciated."
of course, only if you make
much more for them than they pay
you.

out of the alley and into the
sunlight again,
into heavy traffic,
planning the route to your next stop,
the best way, the time-

saver,
you knowing none of the tricks
and to actually think about
all the deliveries that still lie ahead
would lead to
madness.
it's one at a time,
easing in and out of traffic
between other work-driven drivers
also with no concept of danger,
reality, flow or
compassion.
you can feel the despair
escaping from their
machines,
their lives as hopeless and
as numbed as
yours.

you break through the cluster
of them
on your way to the next
stop,
driving through teeming downtown
Los Angeles in 1952,
stinking and hungover,
no time for lunch,
no time for coffee,
you're on route #10,
a new man,
give the new man the
ball-busting route,

see if he can swallow the
whale.

you look down and the
needle is on
red.
almost no gas left.
too fucking bad.
you gun it,
lighting a crushed cigarette with
one hand from a soiled pack of
matches.

shit on the world.

come on in!

welcome to my wormy hell.
the music grinds off-key.
fish eyes watch from the wall.
this is where the last happy shot was
fired.
the mind snaps closed
like a mind snapping
closed.
we need to discover a new will and a new
way.
we're stuck here now
listening to the laughter of the
gods.
my temples ache with the fact of
the facts.
I get up, move about, scratch
myself.
I'm a pawn.
I am a hungry prayer.
my wormy hell welcomes you.
hello. hello there. come in, come on in!
plenty of room here for us all,
sucker.
we can only blame ourselves so
come sit with me in the dark.
it's half-past
nowhere
everywhere.

the bakers of 1935

my mother, father and I
walked to the market
once a week
for our government relief food:
cans of beans, cans of
weenies, cans of hash,
some potatoes, some
eggs.
we carried the supplies
in large shopping
bags.

and as we left the market
we always stopped
outside
where there was a large
window
where we could see the
bakers
kneading
the flour into the
dough.
there were 5 bakers,
large young men
and they stood at
5 large wooden tables
working very hard,
not looking up.
they flipped the dough in
the air
and all the sizes and

designs were
different.

we were always hungry
and the sight of the men
working the dough,
flipping it in the
air was a wondrous
sight, indeed.
but then, it would come time
to leave
and we would walk away
carrying our heavy
shopping bags.

"those men have jobs,"
my father would say.
he said it each time.
every time we watched
the bakers he would say
that.

"I think I've found a new way
to make the hash,"
my mother would say
each time.
or sometimes it was
the weenies.
we ate the eggs all
different ways:
fried, poached, boiled.
one of our favorites was

poached eggs on hash.
but that favorite finally
became almost impossible
to eat.
and the potatoes, we fried
them, baked them, boiled
them.
but the potatoes had a way
of not becoming as tiresome
as the hash, the eggs, the
beans.

one day, arriving home,
we placed all our foodstuffs
on the kitchen counter and
stared at them.
then we turned away.

"I'm going to hold up a
bank!" my father suddenly
said.

"oh no, Henry, please!"
said my mother,
"please don't!"

"we're going to eat some
steak, we're going to eat
steaks until they come out
of our ears!"

"but Henry, you don't have

a gun!"

"I'll hold something in my
coat, I'll pretend it's a gun!"

"I've got a water pistol,"
I said, "you can use that."

my father looked at me.
"you," he said, "SHUT UP!"

I walked outside.
I sat on the back steps.
I could hear them in there
talking but I couldn't quite make it
out.

then I could hear them again, it was
louder.

"I'll find a new way to cook every-
thing!" my mother said.

"I'm going to rob a goddamned
bank!" my father said.

"Henry, *please, please* don't!"
I heard my mother.

I got up from the steps.
walked away into the
afternoon.

secret laughter

the lair of the hunted is
hidden in the last place
you'd ever look
and even if you find it
you won't believe
it's really there
in much the same way
as the average person
will not believe a great painting.

Democracy

the problem, of course, isn't the Democratic System,
it's the
living parts which make up the Democratic System.
the next person you pass on the street,
multiply
him or
her by
3 or 4 or 30 or 40 million
and you will know
immediately
why things remain non-functional
for most of
us.

I wish I had a cure for the chess pieces
we call Humanity . . .

we've undergone any number of political
cures

and we all remain
foolish enough to hope
that the one on the way
NOW
will cure almost
everything.

fellow citizens,
the problem never was the Democratic
System, the problem is

you.

an empire of coins

the legs are gone and the hopes—the lava of outpouring,
and I haven't shaved in sixteen days
but the mailman still makes his rounds and
water still comes out of the faucet and I have a photo of
myself with glazed and milky eyes full of simple music
in golden trunks and 8 oz. gloves when I made the semi-finals
only to be taken out by a German brute who should have been
locked in a cage for the insane and allowed to drink blood.
Now I am insane and stare at the wallpaper as one would stare
at a Dalí (he has lost it) or an early Picasso, and I send
the girls out for beer, the old girls who barely bother to wipe
their asses and say, "well, I guess I won't comb my hair today:
it might bring me luck." well, anyway, they wash the dishes and
chop the wood, and the landlady keeps insisting "let me in,
    I can't
get in, you've got the lock on, and what's all that singing and
cussing in there?" but she only wants a piece of ass while   .
    she pretends
she wants the rent
                    but she's not going to get either one of 'em.
meanwhile the skulls of the dead are full of beetles and
    Shakes-
peare and old football scores like S.C. 16, N.D. 14 on a John
Baker field goal.

I can see the fleet from my window, the sails and the guns, always
the guns poking their eyes in the sky looking for trouble like young
L.A. cops too young to shave, and the younger sailors out
there sex-hungry, trying to act tough, trying to act like men
but really closer to their mother's nipples than to a true evalu-
ation of existence. I say god damn it, that
my legs are gone and the outpourings too. inside my brain

they cut and snip and
                        pour oil
to burn and fire out early dreams.
"darling," says one of the girls, "you've got to snap out of it,
we're running out of MONEY. how do you want
your toast?
                        light or dark?"

a woman's a woman, I say, and I put my binoculars between her
kneecaps and I can see where
empires have fallen.

I wish I had a brush, some paint, some paint and a brush, I say.

"why?" asks one of the
whores.

BECAUSE RATS DON'T LIKE OIL! I scream.

(I can't go on. I don't belong here.) I listen to radio programs and
people's voices talking and I marvel that they can get excited
and interested over nothing and I flick out the lights, I
crash out the lights, and I pull the shades down, I
tear the shades down and I light my last cigar imagining
the dreamjump off the Empire State Building
into the thickheaded bullbrained mob with the hard-on attitude.
already forgotten are the dead of Normandy, Lincoln's
     stringy beard,
all the bulls that have died to flashing red capes,
all the love that has died in real women and real men
while fools have been elevated to the trumpet's succulent sneer
and I have fought red-handed and drunk

in slop-pitted alleys
the bartenders of this rotten land.

and I laugh, I can still laugh, who can't laugh when the
    whole thing
is so ridiculous
                that only the insane, the clowns, the half-wits,
the cheaters, the whores, the horseplayers, the bankrobbers, the
poets . . . are interesting?

in the dark I hear the hands reaching for the last of my money
like mice nibbling at paper, automatic feeders on inbred
helplessness, a false drunken God asleep at the wheel . . .
a quarter rolls across the floor, and I remember all the faces
    and
the football heroes, and everything has meaning, and an editor
writes me, you are good
                but
                  you are too emotional
the way to whip life is to quietly frame the agony,
study it and put it to sleep in the abstract.
is there anything less abstract
                than dying day by day?

The door closes and the last of the great whores are gone
and somehow no matter how they have
killed me, they are all great, and I smoke quietly
thinking of Mexico, the tired horses, of Havana and Spain
and Normandy, of the jabbering insane, of my dear
friends, of no more friends
ever; and the voice of my Mexican buddy saying, "you
    won't die

you won't die in the war, you're too smart, you'll take care
of yourself."

I keep thinking of the bulls. the brave bulls dying every day.
the whores are gone. the bombing has stopped for a minute.

fuck everybody.

what?

sleepy now
at 4 a.m.
I hear the siren
of a white
ambulance,
then a dog
barks
once
in this tough-boy
Christmas
morning.

the American Flag Shirt

now more and more
all these people running around
wearing the American Flag Shirt
and it was more or less once assumed
(I think but I'm not sure)
that wearing an A.F.S. meant to
say you were pissing on
it
but now
they keep making them
and everybody keeps buying them
and wearing them
and the faces are just like
the American Flag Shirt—
this one has this face and that shirt
that one has that shirt and this face—
and somebody's spending money
and somebody's making money
and as the patriots become
more and more fashionable
it'll be nice
when everybody looks around
and finds that they are all patriots now
and therefore
who is there left to
persecute
except their
children?

now she's free

Cleo's going to make it now
she's got her shit together
she split with Barney
Barney wasn't good for her
she got a bigger apartment
furnished it beautifully
and bought a new silver Camaro
she works afternoons in a dance joint
drives 30 miles to the job from
Redondo Beach
goes to night school
helps out at the AIDS clinic
reads the *I Ching*
does Yoga
is living with a 20-year-old boy
eats health food
Barney wasn't good for her
she's got her shit together now
she's into T.M.
but she's the same old fun-loving Cleo
she's painted her nails green
got a butterfly tattoo
I saw her yesterday
in her new silver Camaro
her long blonde hair blowing
in the wind.
poor Barney.
he just doesn't know what he's
missing.

the simple truth

you just don't know how to do it,
you know that,
and you can't do a lot of other
useful things either.
it's the fault of the
way you were raised,
some of it,
and you'll never learn now,
it's too late.
you just can't do certain things.
I could show you how to do them
but you still wouldn't do them
right.
I learned how to do a lot of necessary things
when I was a little girl
and I can still do them now.
I had good parents but
your parents never gave you enough
attention or love
so you never learned how to do
certain simple things.
I know it's not your fault but
I think you should be aware of how
limited you are.

here, let me do that!
now watch me!
see how easy it is!
take your time!
you have no patience!

now look at you!
you're mad, aren't you?
I can tell.
you think I can't tell?

I'm going downstairs now,
my favorite tv program is coming
on.

and don't be mad because
I tell you the simple truth about
yourself.

do you want anything from
downstairs?
a snack?
no?

are you sure?

gold in your eye

I got into my BMW and drove down to my bank to
pick up my American Express Gold Card.

I told the girl at the desk what I
wanted.

"you're Mr. Chinaski," she
said.

"yes, you want some
i.d.?"

"oh no, we know you ..."

I slipped the card into my wallet
went back to parking
got into the BMW (paid for, straight
cash)
and decided to drive down to the liquor store
for a case of fine
wine.

on the way, I further decided to write a poem
about the whole thing: the BMW, the bank, the
Gold Card
just to piss off the
critics
the writers
the readers

who much preferred the old poems about me
sleeping on park benches while

freezing and dying of cheap wine and
malnutrition.

this poem is for those who think that
a man can only be a creative
genius
at the very
edge
even though they never had the
guts to
try it.

a great writer

a great writer remains in bed
shades down
doesn't want to see anyone
doesn't want to write anymore
doesn't want to try anymore;
the editors and publishers wonder:
some say he's insane
some say he's dead;
his wife now answers all the mail:
".. he does not wish to ..."
and some others even walk up and down
outside his house,
look at the pulled-down
shades;
some even go up and ring the
bell.
nobody answers.
the great writer does not want to be
disturbed. perhaps the great writer is not
in? perhaps the great writer has gone
away?

but they all want to know the truth,
to hear his voice, to be told some good
reason for it all.

if he has a reason
he does not reveal it.
perhaps there isn't any
reason?

strange and disturbing arrangements are
made; his books and paintings are quietly
auctioned off;
no new work has appeared now for
years.

yet his public won't accept his
silence—
if he is dead
they want to know; if he is
insane they want to know; if he has a
reason, please tell us!

they walk past his house
write letters
ring the bell
they cannot understand and will not
accept
the way things are.

I rather like
it.

the smoking car

they stop out front here
it looks as if the car is on fire
the smoke blazes blue from the hood and exhaust
the motor sounds like cannon shots
the car humps wildly
one guy gets out,
Jesus, he says, he takes a long drink from a
canvas water bag
and gives the car an eerie look.
the other guy gets out and looks at the car,
Jesus, he says,
and he takes a drink from a pint of whiskey,
then passes the bottle to his
friend.
they both stand and look at the car,
one holding the whiskey, the other the water bag.
they are not dressed in conventional hippie garb
but in natural old clothes
faded, dirty and torn.
a butterfly goes past my window
and they get back in the
car
and it bucks off in low
like a rodeo bronc
they are both laughing
and one has the bottle
tilted . . .

the butterfly is gone
and outside there is a globe of smoke
40 feet in circumference.

first human beings I've seen in Los Angeles
in 15 years.

the shoelace

a woman, a
tire that's flat, a
disease, a
desire; fears in front of you,
fears that hold so still
you can study them
like pieces on a
chessboard . . .
it's not the large things that
send a man to the
madhouse. death he's ready for, or
murder, incest, robbery, fire, flood . . .
no, it's the continuing series of *small* tragedies
that send a man to the
madhouse . . .
not the death of his love
but a shoelace that snaps
with no time left . . .
the dread of life
is that swarm of trivialities
that can kill quicker than cancer
and which are always there—
license plates or taxes
or expired driver's license,
or hiring or firing,
doing it or having it done to you, or
constipation
speeding tickets
rickets or crickets or mice or termites or
roaches or flies or a
broken hook on a
screen, or out of gas

or too much gas,
the sink's stopped up, the landlord's drunk,
the president doesn't care and the governor's
crazy.
lightswitch broken, mattress like a
porcupine;
$105 for a tune-up, carburetor and fuel pump at
Sears Roebuck;
and the phone bill's up and the market's
down
and the toilet chain is
broken,
and the light has burned out—
the hall light, the front light, the back light,
the inner light; it's
darker than hell
and twice as
expensive.
then there's always crabs and ingrown toenails
and people who insist they're
your friends;
there's always that and worse;
leaky faucet, Christ and Christmas;
blue salami, 9 day rains,
50 cent avocados
and purple
liverwurst.

or making it
as a waitress at Norm's on the split shift,
or as an emptier of
bedpans,

or as a carwash or a busboy
or a stealer of old lady's purses
leaving them screaming on the sidewalks
with broken arms at the age of
80.

suddenly
2 red lights in your rearview mirror
and blood in your
underwear;
toothache, and $979 for a bridge
$300 for a gold
tooth,
and China and Russia and America, and
long hair and short hair and no
hair, and beards and no
faces, and plenty of *zigzag* but no
pot, except maybe one to piss in and
the other one around your
gut.

with each broken shoelace
out of one hundred broken shoelaces,
one man, one woman, one
thing
enters a
madhouse.

so be careful
when you
bend over.

self-inflicted wounds

he talked about Steinbeck and Thomas Wolfe and he
wrote like a cross between the two of them
and I lived in a hotel on Figueroa Street
close to the bars
and he lived further uptown in a small room
and we both wanted to be writers
and we'd meet at the public library, sit on the stone
benches and talk about that.
he showed me his short stories and he wrote well, he
wrote better than I did, there was a calm and a
strength in his work that mine did not have.
my stories were jagged, harsh, with self-inflicted wounds.

I showed him all my work but he was more impressed with
my drinking prowess and my worldly attitude

after talking a bit we would go to Clifton's Cafeteria
for our only meal of the day
(for less than a dollar in 1941)
yet
we were in great health.
we lost jobs, found jobs, lost jobs.
mostly we didn't work, we always envisioned we soon
would be receiving regular checks from
The New Yorker, The Atlantic Monthly and
Harper's.

we ran with a gang of young men who didn't envision
anything at all
but they had a gallant lawless charm
and we drank with them and fought with them and
had a hell of a wild good time.

then just like that he joined the Marine Corps.
"I want to prove something to myself" was what he told
me.

he did: right after boot camp the war came and in 3 months
he was dead.
and I promised myself that some day I would write a novel and
    that
I would dedicate it to him.

I have now written 5 novels, all dedicated to others.

you know, you were right, Robert Baun, when you once told
me, "Bukowski, about half of what you say is
bullshit."

Verdi

and
so
we suck on a cigar
and a beer
attempting to mend the love
wounds of the soul.

a beer.

a cigar.

I listen to Verdi
scratch my hindquarters
and
stare out of
a cloud of
blue
smoke.

have you ever been to
Venice?

Madrid?

the stress of continually facing the
lowered
horn
is wearing.

then too
I sometimes think of a
less stressful kind of

love—
it can and should be so
easy
like falling asleep
in a chair or
like a church full of
windows.

sad enough,
I wish only for that careless love
which is sweet
gentle
and which is
now
(like
     this light
     over my head)
there only to serve me
while I
smoke smoke smoke
out of a certain center dressed
in an old brown shirt.

but I am caught under a pile of
bricks;
poetry is shot in the head
and walks down the alley
pissing on its legs.

friends, stop writing of
breathing
in this sky of fire.

small children,
walk well behind us.

but now Verdi
abides with the
wallpaper
with beerlove,
with the taste of wet gold as
my fingers dabble in ashes
as strange young ladies walk outside
my window
dreaming of broomsticks,
palaces
and
blueberry pie.

(uncollected)

the young lady who lives in Canoga Park

she only fucks the ones she doesn't want
to marry.
to the others she says
you've got to marry me.
or maybe she just fucks the ones she wants
to fuck?
she talks about it freely
and lives in the apartment at the end
with a 9-year-old red-haired boy
and a 7-month-old baby.
she gets child support
and when she works
she works in the factories or as a
cocktail waitress.
she has a boyfriend 60 years old
who drinks a jug of wine a day
has a bad leg
and lives at the YMCA.
she smokes dope, mostly grass,
takes pills
wears large dark glasses
and talks talks talks
while not looking at you and
twisting a long beaded necklace with her thin
nervous fingers.
she has a neck like a swan,
could be a movie star,
twice in the madhouse,
a mother in the madhouse,
and a sister in prison.
you never know when she is going to

go mad again and
throw tiny fits
and 3 a.m. phone calls at you.

the kids trundle about the apartment
and she fucks and doesn't fuck,
has an exercise chart on her wall
bends this way and that
touches her toes
leaps
stretches and so
forth. she goes from dope to religion
and from religion back to dope and
from black guys to white guys and from white to
black again.

when she takes off those dark glasses
her eyes are blue
and she tries to smile
as she twists that necklace
around and around.
there are 3 keys on the end of it:
her car key
her apartment key
and one that I've never
asked her about.
she's not given up,
she's not dead yet,
she's hardly even old,
her air conditioner doesn't

work and that's really all I know
about her because I'm one of those
she wants to
marry.

(uncollected)

life of the king

I awaken at 11:30 a.m.
get into my chinos and a clean green shirt
open a Miller's,
and nothing in the mailbox but the
Berkeley Tribe
which I don't subscribe to,
and on KUSC there is organ music
something by Bach
and I leave the door open
stand on the porch
walk out front
hot damn
that air is good
and the sun like golden butter on my
body. no racetrack today, nothing but this
beastly and magic
leisure, rolled cigarette dangling
I scratch my belly in the sun
as Paul Hindemith
rides by on a bicycle,
and down the street a lady in a
very red dress
bends down into a laundry basket
rises
hangs a sheet on a line,
bends again, rises, in all that red,
that red like snake skin
clinging moving flashing
hot damn
I keep looking, and
she sees me
pauses bent over basket

clothespin in mouth
she rises with a pair of pink
panties
smiles around the
clothespin
waves to me.
what's next? rape in the streets?
I wave back,
go in,
sit down at the machine
by the window, and now it's someone's
violin concerto in D,
and a pretty black girl in very tight pants
walking a hound,
they stop outside my window,
look in;
she has on dark shades
and her mouth opens a little, then she and the
    dog
move on.
someone might have bombed cities for this or
sold apples in the
rain.
but whoever is responsible, today I wish to
thank him
all the
way.

my failure

I think of devils in hell
and stare at a
beautiful vase of
flowers
as the woman in my bedroom
angrily switches the light
on and off.
we have had a very bad
argument
and I sit in here smoking
cigarettes from
India
as on the radio an
opera singer's prayers are
not in my
language.
outside, the window to
my left reveals the night
lights of the
city and I only wish
I had the courage to
break through this simple horror
and make things well
again
but my petty anger
prevents
me.

I realize hell is only what we
create,
smoking these cigarettes,
waiting here,

wondering here,
while in the other room
she continues to
sit and
switch the light
on and off,
on and
off.

a boy and his dog

there's Barry in his ripped walking shorts
he's on Thorazine
is 24
looks 38
lives with his mother in the same
apartment building
and they fight like married folk.
he wears dirty white t-shirts
and every time he gets a new dog
he names him "Brownie."
he's like an old woman really.
he'll see me getting into my Volks.
"hey, ya goin' ta work?"
"oh, no Barry, I don't work. I'm going to
the racetrack."
"yeah?"
he walks over to the car window.
"ya heard them last night?"
"who?"
"*them!* they were playin' that shit all night!
I couldn't sleep! they played until one-thirty!
didn't cha hear 'em?"
"no, but I'm in the back, Barry, you're up
front."
we live in east Hollywood among the massage parlors,
adult bookstores and the sex film theatres.
"yeah," says Barry. "I don't know what this neigh-
borhood is comin' to! ya know those other people in
    the front
unit?"
"yes."

"well, I saw through their curtains! and ya know what
they were doin'?"
"no, Barry."
"*this!*" he says and then takes his right forefinger and
pokes it against a vein in his left arm.
"really?"
"yeah! and if it ain't *that,* now we got all these
drunks in the neighborhood!"
"look, Barry, I've got to get to the racetrack."
"aw' right. but ya know what happened?"
"no, Barry."
"a cop stopped me on my Moped. and guess why?"
"speeding?"
"no! he claimed I had to have a license to drive a Moped!
that's stupid! he gave me a ticket! I almost smashed him
in the face!"
"oh yeah?"
"yeah! I almost smashed him!"
"Barry, I've got to make the first race."
"how much does it cost you to get in?"
"four dollars and twenty-five cents."
"I got into the Pomona County Fair for a dollar."
"all right, Barry."
the motor has been running. I put it into first and pull
out. in the rearview mirror I see him walk
back across the lawn.
Brownie is waiting for him,
wagging his tail.
his mother is inside waiting.
maybe Barry will slam her against the refrigerator
thinking about that cop.
or maybe they'll play checkers.

I find the Hollywood freeway
then the Pasadena freeway.
life has been tough on Barry:
he's 24
looks 38
but it all evens out finally:
he's aged a good many other people
too.

liberated woman and liberated man

look there.
the one you considered killing yourself
for.
you saw her the other day
getting out of her car
in the Safeway parking lot.
she was wearing a torn green
dress and old dirty
boots
her face raw with living.
she saw you
so you walked over
and spoke and then
listened.
her hair did not glisten
her eyes and her conversation were
dull.
where was she?
where had she gone?
the one you were going to kill yourself
for?

the conversation finished
she walked into the store
and you looked at her automobile
and even that
which used to drive up and park
in front of your door
with such verve and in a spirit of
adventure
now looked

like a junkyard
joke.

you decide not to shop at
Safeway
you'll drive 6 blocks
east and buy what you need
at Ralphs.

getting into your car
you are quite pleased that
you didn't
kill yourself;
everything is delightful and
the air is clear.
your hands on the wheel,
you grin as you check for traffic in
the rearview mirror.

my man, you think,
you've saved yourself
for somebody else, but
who?

a slim young creature walks by
in a miniskirt and sandals
showing a marvelous leg.
she's going in to shop at Safeway
too.

you turn off the engine and
follow her in.

small talk

all right, while we are gently celebrating tonight
and while crazy classical music leaps at me from
my small radio, I light a fresh cigar
and realize that I am still very much alive and that
the 21st century is almost upon me!

I walk softly now toward 5 a.m. this dark night.
my 5 cats have been in and out, looking after
me, I have petted them, spoken to them, they
are full of their own private fears wrought by previous
centuries of cruelty and abuse
but I think that they love me as much as they
can, anyhow, what I am trying to say here
is that writing is just as exciting and mad and
just as big a gamble for me as it ever was, because Death
after all these years
walks around in the room with me now and speaks softly,
asking, do you still think that you are a genuine
writer? are you pleased with what you've done?
listen, let me have one of those
cigars.

help yourself, motherfucker, I say.

Death lights up and we sit quietly for a time.
I can feel him here with me.

don't you long for the ferocity
of youth? He finally asks.

not so much, I say.

but don't you regret those things
that have been lost?

not at all, I say.

don't you miss, He asks slyly, the young girls
climbing through your window?

all they brought was bad news, I tell him.

but the *illusion,* He says, don't you miss the
illusion?

hell yes, don't you? I ask.

I have no illusions, He says sadly.

sorry, I forgot about that, I say, then walk
to the window
unafraid and strangely satisfied
to watch the warm dawn
unfold.

the crunch

too much
too little

too fat
too thin
or nobody.

laughter or
tears

haters
lovers

strangers with faces like
the backs of
thumb tacks

armies running through
streets of blood
waving winebottles
bayoneting and fucking
virgins.

or an old guy in a cheap room
with a photograph of M. Monroe.

there is a loneliness in this world so great
that you can see it in the slow movement of
the hands of a clock.

people so tired
mutilated
either by love or no love.

people just are not good to each other
one on one

the rich are not good to the rich
the poor are not good to the poor.

we are afraid.

our educational system tells us
that we can all be
big-ass winners.

it hasn't told us
about the gutters
or the suicides.

or the terror of one person
aching in one place
alone

untouched
unspoken to

watering a plant.

people are not good to each other.
people are not good to each other.
people are not good to each other.

I suppose they never will be.
I don't ask them to be.

but sometimes I think about
it.

the beads will swing
the clouds will cloud
and the killer will behead the child
like taking a bite out of an ice cream cone.

too much
too little
too fat
too thin
or nobody

more haters than lovers.

people are not good to each other.
perhaps if they were
our deaths would not be so sad.

meanwhile I look at young girls
stems
flowers of chance.

there must be a way.

surely there must be a way we have not yet
thought of.

who put this brain inside of me?

it cries
it demands
it says that there is a chance.

it will not say
"no."

funhouse

I drive to the beach at night
in the winter
and sit and look at the burned-down amusement pier
wonder why they just let it sit there
in the water.
I want it out of there,
blown up,
vanished,
erased;
that pier should no longer sit there
with madmen sleeping inside
the burned-out guts of the funhouse . . .
it's awful, I say, blow the damn thing up,
get it out of my eyes,
that tombstone in the sea.

the madmen can find other holes
to crawl into.
I used to walk that pier when I was 8
years old.

the poetry reading

at high noon
at a small college near the beach
sober
the sweat running down my arms
a spot of sweat on the table
I flatten it with my finger
blood money   blood money
my god they must think I love this like the others
but it's for bread and beer and rent
blood money
I'm tense   lousy   feel bad
poor people   I'm failing   I'm failing

a woman gets up
walks out
slams the door

a dirty poem
somebody told me not to read dirty poems
here

it's too late.

my eyes can't see some lines
I read it
out—
desperate trembling
lousy

they can't hear my voice
and I say,

I quit, that's it, I'm
finished.

and later in my room
there's scotch and beer:
the blood of a coward.

this then
will be my destiny:
scrabbling for pennies in dark tiny halls
reading poems I have long since become tired
of.

and I used to think
that men who drove buses
or cleaned out latrines
or murdered men in alleys were
fools.

somebody

god I got the sad blue blues,
this woman sat there and she
said
are you really Charles

               Bukowski?
and I said

        forget that
I do not feel good
I've got the sad sads
all I want to do is
fuck you

and she laughed
she thought I was being
clever .
and O I just looked up her long slim legs of heaven
I saw her liver and her quivering intestine
I saw Christ in there
jumping to a folk-rock

all the long lines of starvation within me
rose
and I walked over
and grabbed her on the couch
ripped her dress up around her face

and I didn't care
rape or the end of the earth
one more time
to be there
anywhere
real

yes
her panties were on the
floor
and my cock went in
my cock my god my cock went in

I was Charles
Somebody.

the colored birds

it is a highrise apt. next door
and he beats her at night and she screams and nobody stops it
and I see her the next day
standing in the driveway with curlers in her hair
and she has her huge buttocks jammed into black
slacks and she says, standing in the sun,
"god damn it, 24 hours a day in this place, I never go anywhere!"

then he comes out, proud, the little matador,
a pail of shit, his belly hanging over his bathing trunks—
he might have been a handsome man once, might have,
now they both stand there and he says,
"I think I'm goin' for a swim."
she doesn't answer and he goes to the pool and
jumps into the fishless, sandless water, the peroxide-codeine water,
and I stand by the kitchen window drinking coffee
trying to unboil the fuzzy, stinking picture—
after all, you can't live elbow to elbow to people without wanting to
draw a number on them.
every time my toilet flushes they can hear it. every time they
go to bed I can hear them.

soon she goes inside and then comes out with 2 colored birds
in a cage. I don't know what they are. they don't talk. they
just move a little, seeming to twitch their tail-feathers and
shit. that's all they do.
she stands there looking at them.
he comes out: the little tuna, the little matador, out of the pool,
a dripping unbeautiful white, the cloth of his wet suit gripping.
"get those birds in the house!"
"but the birds need sun!"
"I said, get those birds in the house!"

"the birds are gonna die!"
"you listen to me, I said, GET THOSE BIRDS IN THE HOUSE!"
she bends and lifts them, her huge buttocks in the black slacks
looking so sad.
he slams the door behind them. then I hear it.
BAM!
        she screams
                BAM! BAM!
                      she screams
                              then: BAM!
                                    and she screams.

I pour another coffee and decide that that's a new
one: he usually only beats her at
night. it takes a man to beat his wife night and
day. although he doesn't look like much
he's one of the few real men around
here.

poem for personnel managers:

An old man asked me for a cigarette
and I carefully dealt out two.
"Been lookin' for job. Gonna stand
in the sun and smoke."

He was close to rags and rage
and he leaned against death.
It was a cold day, indeed, and trucks
loaded and heavy as old whores
banged and tangled on the streets . . .

We drop like planks from a rotting floor
as the world strives to unlock the bone
that weights its brain.
(God is a lonely place without steak.)

We are dying birds
we are sinking ships—
the world rocks down against us
and we
throw out our arms
and we
throw out our legs
like the death kiss of the centipede:
but they kindly snap our backs
and call our poison "politics."

Well, we smoked, he and I—little men
nibbling fish-head thoughts . . .

All the horses do not come in,
and as you watch the lights of the jails

and hospitals wink on and out,
and men handle flags as carefully as babies,
remember this:

you are a great-gutted instrument of
heart and belly, carefully planned—
so if you take a plane for Savannah,
take the best plane;
or if you eat chicken on a rock,
make it a very special animal.
(You call it a bird; I call birds
flowers.)

And if you decide to kill somebody,
make it anybody and not somebody:
some men are made of more special, precious
parts: do not kill
if you will
a president or a King
or a man
behind a desk—
these have heavenly longitudes
enlightened attitudes.

If you decide,
take us
who stand and smoke and glower;
we are rusty with sadness and
feverish
with climbing broken ladders.

Take us:
    we were never children
    like your children.
    We do not understand love songs
    like your inamorata.

Our faces are cracked linoleum,
cracked through with the heavy, sure
feet of our masters.

We are shot through with carrot tops
and poppyseed and tilted grammar;
we waste days like mad blackbirds
and pray for alcoholic nights.
Our silk-sick human smiles wrap around
us like somebody else's confetti:
we do not even belong to the Party.

We are a scene chalked-out with the
sick white brush of Age.

We smoke, asleep as a dish of figs.
We smoke, dead as a fog.

Take us.

A bathtub murder
or something quick and bright; our names
in the papers.

Known, at last, for a moment
to millions of careless and grape-dull eyes

that hold themselves private
to only flicker and flame
at the poor cracker-barrel jibes
of their conceited, pampered correct comedians.

Known, at last, for a moment,
as they will be known
and as you will be known
by an all-gray man on an all-gray horse
who sits and fondles a sword
longer than the night
longer than the mountain's aching backbone
longer than all the cries
that have a-bombed up out of throats
and exploded in a newer, less-planned
land.

We smoke and the clouds do not notice us.
A cat walks by and shakes Shakespeare off of his back.
Tallow, tallow, candle like wax: our spines
are limp and our consciousness burns
guilelessly away
the remaining wick life has
doled out to us.

An old man asked me for a cigarette
and told me his troubles
and this
is what he said:
that Age was a crime
and that Pity picked up the marbles

and that Hatred picked up the
cash.

He might have been your father
or mine.

He might have been a sex-fiend
or a saint.

But whatever he was,
he was condemned
and we stood in the sun and
smoked
and looked around
in our leisure
to see who was next in
line.

my fate

like the fox
I run with the hunted
and if I'm not
the happiest man
on earth
I'm surely the
luckiest man
alive.

(uncollected)

my atomic stockpile

I cleaned my place the other day
first time in ten years
and found 100 rejected poems:
I fastened them all to a clipboard
(much bad reading).

now I will clean their teeth
fill their cavities
give them eye and ear examinations
weigh them
offer blood transfusions
then send them out again into the
sick world of posey.
either that
or I must burn down your cities,
rape your women,
murder your men,
enslave your children.

every time I clean my room
the world trembles in the balance.
that's why I only do it once every
ten years.

(uncollected)

271

Bruckner (2)

Bruckner wasn't bad
even though he got down
on his knees
and proclaimed Wagner
the master.

it saddens me, I guess,
in a small way
because while Wagner was
hitting all those homers
Bruckner was sacrificing
the runners to second
and he knew it.

and I know that
mixing baseball metaphors with classical
music
will not please the purists
either.

I prefer Ruth to most of his teammates
but I appreciate those others who did
the best they could
and kept on doing it
even when they knew they
were second best.

this is your club fighter
your back-up quarterback
the unknown jock who sometimes
brings one in
at 40-to-one.

this was Bruckner.

there are times when we should
remember
the strange courage
of the second-rate
who refuse to quit
when the nights
are black and long and sleepless
and the days are without
end.

hello, how are you?

this fear of being what they are:
dead.

at least they are not out on the street, they
are careful to stay indoors, those
pasty mad who sit alone before their TV sets,
their lives full of canned, mutilated laughter.

their ideal neighborhood
of parked cars
of little green lawns
of little homes
the little doors that open and close
as their relatives visit
throughout the holidays
the doors closing
behind the dying who die so slowly
behind the dead who are still alive
in your quiet average neighborhood
of winding streets
of agony
of confusion
of horror
of fear
of ignorance.

a dog standing behind a fence.

a man silent at the window.

vacancy

sun-stroked women
without men
on a Santa Monica Monday;
the men are working or in jail
or insane;
one girl floats in a rubber suit,
waiting . . .
houses slide off the edges of cliffs
and down into the sea.
the bars are empty
the lobster eating houses are empty;
it's a recession, they say,
the good days are
over.
you can't tell an unemployed man
from an artist any more,
they all look alike
and the women look the same,
only a little more desperate.

we stop at a hippie hole
in Topanga Canyon . . .
and wait, wait, wait;
the whole area of the canyon and the beach
is listless
useless
VACANCY, it says, PEOPLE WANTED.

the wood has no fire
the sea is dirty
the hills are dry

the temples have no bells
love has no bed

sun-stroked women without men

one sailboat

life drowned.

batting slump

the sun slides down through the shades.
I have a pair of black shoes and a pair of
brown shoes.
I can hardly remember the girls of my youth.
there is numb blood pulsing through the
falcon and the hyena and the pimp
and there's no escaping this unreasonable
sorrow.
there's crabgrass and razor wire and the snoring
of my cat.
there are lifeguards sitting in canvas-back chairs
with salt rotting under their toenails.
there's the hunter with eyes like rose
petals.
sorrow, yes, it pulls at me
I don't know why.
avenues of despair slide into my ears.
the worms won't sing.
the Babe swings again
missing a 3-and-2 pitch
twisting around himself
leaning over his
whiskey gut.
cows give milk
dentists pull teeth
thermometers work.

I can sing the blues
it doesn't cost a dime and
when I lay down tonight
pull up the covers
there's the dark factor

there's the unknown factor
there's this manufactured
staggering
black
empty
space.

I got to hit one out of here
pretty soon.

bang bang

absolutely sesamoid
said the skeleton
shoving his chalky foot
upon my desk,
and that was it,
bang bang,
he looked at me,
and it was my bone body
and I was what remained,
and there was a newspaper
on my desk
and somebody folded the newspaper
and I folded,
I was the newspaper
under somebody's arm
and the sheet of me
had eyes
and I saw the skeleton
watching
and just before the door closed
I saw a man who looked
partly like Napoleon,
partly like Hitler,
fighting with my skeleton,
then the door closed
and we went down the steps
and outside
and I was under
the arm
of a fat little man
who knew nothing
and I hated him

for his indifference
to fact, how I hated him
as he unfolded me
in the subway
and I fell against the back
of an old woman.

the pleasures of the damned

the pleasures of the damned
are limited to brief moments
of happiness:
like the eyes in the look of a dog,
like a square of wax,
like a fire taking the city hall,
the county,
the continent,
like fire taking the hair
of maidens and monsters;
and hawks buzzing in peach trees,
the sea running between their claws,
Time
drunk and damp,
everything burning,
everything wet,
everything fine.

one more good one

to be writing poetry at the age of 50
like a schoolboy,
surely, I must be crazy;
racetracks and booze and arguments
with the landlord;
watercolor paintings under the bed
with dirty socks;
a bathtub full of trash
and a garbage can lined with
underground newspapers;
a record player that doesn't work,
a radio that doesn't work,
and I don't work—
I sit between 2 lamps,
bottle on the floor
begging a 20-year-old typewriter
to say something, in a way and
well enough
so they won't confuse me
with the more comfortable
practitioners;
this is certainly not a game for
flyweights or Ping-Pong players—
all arguments to the contrary.

—but once you get the taste, it's good to get your
teeth into
words. I forgive those who
can't quit.
I forgive myself.
this is where the *action* is,
this is the hot horse that

comes in.
there's no grander fort
no better flag
no better woman
no better way; yet there's much else to say—
there seems as much hell in it as
magic; death gets as close as any lover has,
closer,
you know it like your right hand
like a mark on the wall
like your daughter's name,
you know it like the face on the corner
newsboy,
and you sit there with flowers and houses
with dogs and death and a boil on the neck,
you sit down and do it again and again
the machinegun chattering by the window
as the people walk by
as you sit in your undershirt,
50, on an indelicate March evening,
as their faces look in and help you write the next 5
lines,
as they walk by and say,
"the old man in the window, what's the deal with
him?"
—fucked by the muse, friends,
thank you—
and I roll a cigarette with one hand
like the old bum
I am, and then thank and curse the gods
alike,
lean forward

drag on the cigarette
think of the good fighters
like poor Hem, poor Beau Jack, poor Sugar Ray,
poor Kid Gavilan, poor Villon, poor Babe, poor
Hart Crane, poor
me, hahaha.

I lean forward,
redhot ash
falling on my wrists,
teeth into the word.
crazy at the age of 50,
I send it
home.

the little girls hissed

since my last name was Fuch, he said to Raymond, you can
believe the school yard was tough: they put itching
powder down my neck, threw gravel at me, stung me
with rubber bands in class, and outside they called
me names, well, one name mainly, over and over,
and on top of all that my parents were poor, I wore
cardboard in my shoes to fill in the holes in the
soles, my pants were patched, my shirts thread-
bare; and even my teachers ganged up
on me, they slammed my
palm with rulers and sent me to the principal's office as
if I was really guilty of something;
and, of course, the abuse kept coming from my classmates;
I was stoned, beaten, pissed on;
the little girls hissed and stuck their tongues out
at me . . .

Fuch's wife smiled sadly at Raymond: my poor darling husband had
    such a *terrible* childhood!
(she was so beautiful it almost stunned one to look at
her.)

Fuch looked at Raymond: hey, your glass is empty.

yeah, said Raymond.

Fuch touched a button and the English butler silently
glided in. he nodded respectfully to Raymond and in his
beautiful accent asked, another drink, sir?

yes, please, Raymond answered.

the butler went off to prepare the drink.

what hurt most, of course, continued Fuch, was the name-
calling.

Raymond asked, have you never forgotten it?

I did for a while, but then strangely I began to
miss the abuse . . .

the butler returned carrying Raymond's
drink on a silver tray.

here is your drink, sir, said the butler.

thank you, said Raymond, taking it off the tray.

o.k., Paul, Fuch said to the butler, you can
start now.

now? asked the butler.

now, came the answer.

the butler stood in front of Fuch and screamed:
fucky-boy! fucky-baby! fuck-face! fuck-brain!
where did your name come from, fuck-head?
how come you're such a fuck-up?
etc. . . .

they all started laughing uncontrollably
as the butler delivered his tirade in that
beautiful British accent.

they couldn't stop laughing, they fell out of their
chairs and got down on the rug, pounding it and
laughing, Fuch, his lovely young wife and Raymond
in that sprawling mansion overlooking the shining sea.

ha ha ha ha ha, ha ha

monkey feet
small and blue
walking toward you
as the back of a building falls off
and an airplane chews the white sky,
doom is like the handle of a pot,
it's there,
know it,
have ice in your tea,
marry,
have children, visit your
dentist,
do not scream at night
even if you feel like screaming,
count ten
make love to your wife,
or if your wife isn't there
if there isn't anybody there
count 20,
get up and walk to the kitchen
if you have a kitchen
and sit there sweating
at 3 a.m. in the morning
monkey feet
small and blue
walking toward you.

thoughts from a stone bench in Venice

I sit on this bench and look
at the sea and the freaks and the
lovers.

I need new eyes a new mouth new
pillows, a new woman.

every old stud with half an eye in
his head loves to charm and ride
a new young calf.

when I think of womenless men mowing their
Saturday lawns and playing football,
baseball, basketball with their sons
I feel like vomiting into the far
horizon.

the family stinks of Christ
and the American Stock Exchange.
the family stinks of safety and
numbness and Thanksgiving turkeys.
the family stinks of airless packed
automobiles driving through
redwood forests.

I need new eyes a new woman new
ankles a new voice new betrayals.

I don't want a long funeral
procession when I die.
I want to move on without weight
or obligation.

I want just the sullen darkness I want
a tomb like this night now:
me here undiluted —
solid, cranky, immaculate.
I hold fast to me. that's all there
is.

(uncollected)

**scene in a tent outside the cotton fields
of Bakersfield:**

we fought for 17 days inside that tent
thrusting and counter-thrusting
but finally she got away
and I walked outside
and spit
in the dirty sand.

Abdullah, I said, why don't you
wash your shorts? you've been
wearing the same
shorts
for 17 years.

Effendi, he said, it's the sun,
the sun cleans everything. what
went with the girl?

I don't know if I couldn't
please her
or if I couldn't
catch her. she was
pretty young.

what did she cost, Effendi?

17 camel.

he whistled through his broken
teeth. aren't you going
to catch her?

howinthehell how? can I get
my camels back?

you are an American, he said.

I walked into the tent
fell upon the ground
and held my head
within
my hands.

suddenly she burst within
the tent
laughing madly,
Americano,
  Americano!

please
    go away
I said quietly.

men are, she said sitting down and rolling down
her stockings, some parts titty and some parts
tiger. you don't mind
if I roll down
my stockings?

I don't mind, I said,
if you roll down the top
of your dress. whores are

always rolling down
their hose. please
go away. I read where
the cruiser crew passed the helmet
for the red cross; I think I'll
have them pass it
to brace your flabby
butt.

have 'em pass the helmet twice, dad,
she said, howcum you don't love me
no more?

I been thinking, I said,
how can Love have a urinary tract
and distended bowels?
pack up, daughter, and flow,
maneuver out of the mansions
of my sight!

you forget, daddy-o, we're in
my tent!

oh, Christ, I said, the trivialities
of private ownership! where's my
hat?

you were wearing a towel, dad, but
kiss me, daddy, hold me in your arms!

I walked over and mauled her breasts.

I drink too much beer, she said,
I can't help it if I
piss.

we fucked for 17 days.

3:16 and one half . . .

here I'm supposed to be a great poet
and I'm sleepy in the afternoon
here I am aware of death like a giant bull
charging at me
and I'm sleepy in the afternoon
here I'm aware of wars and men fighting in the ring
and I'm aware of good food and wine and good women
and I'm sleepy in the afternoon
I'm aware of a woman's love
and I'm sleepy in the afternoon,
I lean into the sunlight behind a yellow curtain
I wonder where the summer flies have gone
I remember the most bloody death of Hemingway
and I'm sleepy in the afternoon.

some day I won't be sleepy in the afternoon
some day I'll write a poem that will bring volcanoes
to the hills out there
but right now I'm sleepy in the afternoon
and somebody asks me, "Bukowski, what time is it?"
and I say, "3:16 and a half."
I feel very guilty, I feel obnoxious, useless,
demented, I feel
sleepy in the afternoon,
they are bombing churches, o.k., that's o.k.,
the children ride ponies in the park, o.k., that's o.k.,
the libraries are filled with thousands of books of knowledge,
great music sits inside the nearby radio
and I am sleepy in the afternoon,
I have this tomb within myself that says,
ah, let the others do it, let them win,

let me sleep,
wisdom is in the dark
sweeping through the dark like brooms,
I'm going where the summer flies have gone,
try to catch me.

a literary discussion

Markov claims I am trying
to stab his soul
but I'd prefer his wife.

I put my feet on the coffee table
and he says,
I don't mind you putting
your feet on the coffee table
except that the legs are wobbly
and the thing
will fall apart
any minute.

I leave my feet on the table
but I'd prefer his wife.

I would rather, says Markov,
entertain a ditchdigger
or a news vendor
because they are kind enough
to observe the decencies
even though
they don't know
Rimbaud from rat poison.

my empty beercan
rolls to the floor.

that I must die
bothers me less than
a straw, says Markov,
my part of the game

is that I must live
the best I can.

I grab his wife as she walks by,
and then her can is against my belly,
and she has fine knees and breasts
and I kiss her.

it is not so bad, being old, he says,
a calmness sets in, but here's the catch:
to keep calmness and deadness
separate; never to look upon youth
as inferior because you are old,
never to look upon age as wisdom
because you have experience. a
man can be old and a fool—
many are, a man can be young
and wise—few are. a—

for Christ's all sake, I wailed,
shut up!

he walked over and got his cane and
walked out.

you've hurt his feelings, she said,
he thinks you are a great poet.

he's too slick for me, I said,
he's too wise.

I had one of her breasts out.
it was a monstrous
beautiful
thing.

butterflies

I believe in earning one's own way
but I also believe in the unexpected
gift
and it is a wondrous thing
when a woman who has read your works
(or parts of them, anyhow)
offers her self to you
out of the blue
a total
stranger.

such an offer
such a communion
must be taken as
holy.

the hands
the fingers
the hair
the smell
the light.

one would like to be strong enough
to turn them away

those butterflies.

I believe in earning one's own way
but I also believe in the unexpected gift.

I have no shame.

we deserve one
another

those butterflies
who flutter to my tiny
flame
and
me.

the great escape

listen, he said, you ever seen a bunch of crabs in a
bucket?
no, I told him.
well, what happens is that now and then one crab
will climb up on top of the others
and begin to climb toward the top of the bucket,
then, just as he's about to escape
another crab grabs him and pulls him back
down.
really? I asked.
really, he said, and this job is just like that, none
of the others want anybody to get out of
here. that's just the way it is
in the postal service!
I believe you, I said.

just then the supervisor walked up and said,
you fellows were talking.
there is no talking allowed on this
job.

I had been there eleven and one-half
years.

I got up off my stool and climbed right up the
supervisor
and then I reached up and pulled myself right
out of there.

it was so easy it was unbelievable.
but none of the others followed me.

and after that, whenever I had crab legs
I thought about that place.
I must have thought about that place
maybe 5 or 6 times

before I switched to lobster.

my friend William

my friend William is a fortunate man:
he lacks the imagination to suffer

he kept his first job
his first wife

can drive a car 50,000 miles
without a brake job

he dances like a swan
and has the prettiest blankest eyes
this side of El Paso

his garden is a paradise
the heels of his shoes are always level
and his handshake is firm

people love him

when my friend William dies
it will hardly be from madness or cancer

he'll walk right past the devil
and into heaven

you'll see him at the party tonight
grinning
over his martini

blissful and delightful
as some guy
fucks his wife in the
bathroom.

safe

the house next door makes me
sad.
both man and wife rise early and
go to work.
they arrive home in early evening.
they have a young boy and a girl.
by 9 p.m. all the lights in the house
are out.
the next morning both man and
wife rise early again and go to
work.
they return in early evening.
by 9 p.m. all the lights are
out.

the house next door makes me
sad.
the people are nice people, I
like them.

but I feel them drowning.
and I can't save them.

they are surviving.
they are not
homeless.

but the price is
terrible.

sometimes during the day
I will look at the house

and the house will look at
me
and the house will
weep, yes, it does, I
feel it.

the house is sad for the people living
there
and I am too
and we look at each other
and cars go up and down the
street,
boats cross the harbor
and the tall palms poke
at the sky
and tonight at 9 p.m.
the lights will go out,
and not only in that
house
and not only in this
city.
safe lives hiding,
almost
stopped,
the breathing of
bodies and little
else.

starve, go mad, or kill yourself

I'm not going to die
easy;
I've sat on your suicide beds
in some of the worst
holes in America,
penniless and mad I've been,
I mean, insane, you know;
big tears, each one the size of your bastard hearts,
flowing down,
roaches crawling into my shoes,
one dirty 40-watt lightbulb overhead
and a room that smelled like piss;
while your rich
your falsely famous
laughed in safe stale places
far away,
you gave me a suicide bed and two choices,
no three:
starve, go mad, or kill yourself.

for now enjoy your trips to Paris where
you consort with great painters and dupes,
but I am getting ready for your eyes and your brain and
your dirty dishwater souls;
you men who have created a pigpen for millions
to choke soundlessly in—
from India to Los Angeles
from Paris to the tits of the Nile—
you're fucked up
you rich you warty you insecure you pricky
damned imbecile pasty white
idiots with your starched shirts and your starched wives and, yes yes,

your starched lives,
get away get away
get away
go to Paris
while you can
while I let you.

the jolly damned man with the hoe (see Markham)
didn't answer the call,
but your children will be raped and your pigs will be eaten
and the skies will burn black with crows and your cries,
as you answer for centuries of
unbearable indignity and bullshit.
you will be dealt with
we know you now
we've known you forever;
the might of the timorous
flies forth like a tremendous and ever beautiful swan,
no shit, friend,
look up look up look up look up
the jolly damned man with the hoe
is now flying over Milwaukee
grinning
more lovely than the sun
more graceful than all the ugly wounds
more real than you
or I or anything.

(uncollected)

the beautiful lady

we are gathered here now
to bury her in this
poem.

she did not marry an unemployed wino who
beat her every
night.

her several children will never wear
snot-stained shirts
or torn dresses.

the beautiful lady
simply
calmly
died.

and may the clean dirt of this poem
bury
her.

her and her womb
and her jewels
and her combs and her
poems

and her pale blue eyes
and her
grinning
rich
frightened
husband.

my life as a sitcom

stepped into the wrong end of the Jacuzzi and twisted my
right leg which was bad to begin with, then that night got drunk
with a tv writer and an actor, something about using my
life to make a sitcom and luckily that fell through and the next
day at the track I get a box seat in the dining area, get a
menu and a glass of water, my leg is really paining me, I
can barely walk to the betting window and back, then
about the 3rd race the waiter rushes by, asks, "can I
borrow your menu?" but he doesn't wait for an answer,
he just grabs it and runs off.
a couple of races go by, I fight through my pain and continue to
make my bets, get back, sit down just as the waiter rushes by again.
he grabs all my silverware and my napkin and runs off.
"HEY!" I yell but he's gone.
all around me people are eating, drinking and laughing.
I check my watch after the 6th race and it is 4:30 p.m.
I haven't been served yet and I'm 72 years old with
a hangover and a leg from hell.
I pull myself to my feet by the edge of the table and manage
to hobble about looking for the maitre d'. I see him down
a far aisle and wave him in.
"can I speak to you?" I ask.
"certainly, sir!"
"look, it's the 7th race, they took my menu and my silver-
ware and I haven't been served yet."
"we'll take care of it right away, sir!"
well, the 7th race went, the 8th race went, and
still no service.
I purchase my ticket for the 9th race and take the
escalator down.
on the first floor, I purchase a sandwich.
I eat it going down another escalator to the parking lot.

the valet laughs as I slowly work my leg into the
car, making a face of pain as I do so.
"got a gimpy leg there, huh, Hank?" he asks.
I pull out, make it to the boulevard and onto the
freeway which immediately begins to slow down because
of a 3-car crash ahead.

I snap on the radio in time to find that my horse
has run out in the 9th.
a flash of pain shoots up my right leg.
I decide to tell my wife about my
misfortunes at the track
even though I know she will respond
by telling me that everything as always
was completely my fault
but when a man is in pain he can't think right,
he only asks for
more.

and
gets it.

who needs it?

see this poem?
it was
written without drinking.
I don't need to drink
to write.
I can write without
drinking.
my wife says I can.
I say that maybe I can.
I'm not drinking
and I'm writing.
see this poem?
it was
written without drinking.
who needs a drink now?

probably the reader.

riots

I've watched this city burn twice
in my lifetime
and the most notable event
was the reaction of the
politicians in the
aftermath
as they
proclaimed the injustice of
the system
and demanded a new
deal for the hapless and the
poor.

nothing was corrected last
time.
nothing will be changed this
time.

the poor will remain poor.
the unemployed will remain
so.
the homeless will remain
homeless

and the politicians,
fat upon the land, will thrive
forever.

those marvelous lunches

when I was in grammar school
my parents were
poor
and in my lunch bag there was
only a peanut butter sandwich.

Richardson didn't have a
lunch bag,
he had a lunch pail with
compartments, a
thermos full of
chocolate milk.
he had ham sandwiches,
sliced beef sandwiches,
apples, bananas, a
pickle and a large bag of
potato chips.

I sat next to Richardson
as we ate.
his potato chips looked
so good—
large and crisp as the
sun blazed upon
them.

"you want some potato
chips?" he would
ask.
and each day
I would eat some.

as I went to school each
day
my thoughts
were on Richardson's
lunch, and especially
those chips.

each morning as we
studied in class
I thought about
lunchtime.
and sitting next to
Richardson.

Richardson was the
sissy and the other
boys looked down
on me
for eating with
him
but I
didn't care.
it was the potato
chips, I couldn't
help myself.

"you want some
potato chips, Henry?"
he would
ask.

"yes."

the other boys got
after me
when Richardson
wasn't
around.

"hey, who's your
sissy friend?
you one
too?"

I didn't like that
but the potato
chips were more
important.

after a while
nobody spoke to
me.

sometimes I ate
one of Richardson's
apples
or I got half a
pickle.

I was always
hungry.
Richardson was
fat,
he had a big
belly

and fleshy
thighs.
he was the only
friend I had in
grammar
school.
we seldom spoke
to each
other.
we just sat
together at
lunchtime.

I walked home with
him after school
and often some of
the boys would
follow us.

they
would gather around
Richardson,
gang up on him,
push him around,
knock him
down
again and
again.

after they were
finished
I would go

pick up his lunch
pail,
which was
spilled on its
side
with the lid
open.

I would place the
thermos back
inside,
close the
lid.

then I would
carry the pail as
I walked Richardson
back to his
house.

we never spoke.

as we got to his door
I would hand him
the lunch
pail.

then the door would
close and he would
be gone.

I was the only friend
he had.

sissies live a hard
life.

The Look:

I once bought a toy rabbit
at a department store
and now he sits and ponders
me with pink sheer eyes:

He wants golf balls and glass
walls.
I want quiet thunder.

Our disappointment sits between us.

the big one

he buys 5 cars a month, details them, waxes and buffs
them out, then
resells them at a profit of one or two grand.

he has a nice Jewish wife and he tells me that he
bangs her until the walls shake.

he wears a red cap, squints in the light, has a regular
job besides the car gig.

I have no idea of what he is trying to accomplish and maybe he
doesn't either.

he's a nicer fellow than most, always good to see him,
we laugh, say a few bright lines.

but
each time
after I see him
I get the blues for him, for me, for all of us:

for want of something to do

we keep slaying our small dragons

as the big one waits.

the genius

this man sometimes forgets who
he is.
sometimes he thinks he's the
Pope.

other times he thinks he's a
hunted rabbit
and hides under the
bed.

then
all at once
he'll recapture total
clarity
and begin creating
works of
art.

then he'll be all right
for some
time.

then, say,
he'll be sitting with his
wife
and 3 or 4 other
people
discussing various
matters

he will be charming,
incisive,
original.

then he'll do
something
strange.

like once
he stood up
unzipped
and began
pissing
on the
rug.

another time
he ate a paper
napkin.

and there was
the time
he got into his
car
and drove it
backwards
all the way to
the
grocery store
and back
again
backwards

the other motorists
screaming at
him
but he
made it
there and
back
without
incident
and without
being
stopped
by a patrol
car.

but he's best
as the
Pope
and his
Latin
is very
good.

his works of
art
aren't that
exceptional
but they allow him
to
survive
and to live with
a series of

19-year-old
wives
who
cut his hair
his toenails
bib
tuck and
feed
him.

he wears everybody
out
but
himself.

about the PEN conference

take a writer away from his typewriter
and all you have left
is
the sickness
which started him
typing
in the
beginning.

what a man I was

I shot off his left ear
then his right,
and then tore off his belt buckle
with hot lead,
and then
I shot off everything that counts
and when he bent over
to pick up his drawers
and his marbles
(poor critter)
I fixed it so he wouldn't have
to straighten up
no more.

Ho Hum.
I went in for a fast snort
and one guy *seemed*
to be looking at me sideways,
and that's how he died—
sideways,
lookin' at me
and clutchin'
for his marbles.

Sight o' blood made me kinda
hungry.
Had a ham sandwich.
Played a couple of sentimental songs . . .
Shot out all the lights
and strolled outside.
Didn't seem to be no one around

so I shot my horse
(poor critter).

Then I saw the Sheerf
a standin' at the end a' the road
and he was shakin'
like he had the Saint Vitus' dance;
it was a real sorrowful sight
so I slowed him to a quiver
with the first slug
and mercifully stiffened him
with the second.

Then I laid on my back awhile
and I shot out the stars one by one
and then
I shot out the moon
and then I walked around
and shot out every light
in town,
and pretty soon it began to get dark
real dark
the way I like it;
just can't stand to sleep
with no light shinin'
on my face.

I laid down and dreamt
I was a little boy again
a playin' with my toy six-shooter
and winnin' all the marble games,

and when I woke up
my guns was gone
and I was all bound hand and foot
just like somebody
was scared a me

and they was slippin'
a noose around my ugly neck
just as if they
meant to hang me,
and some guy was pinnin'
a real pretty sign
on my shirt:
there's a law for you
and a law for me
and a law that hangs
from the foot of a tree.

Well, pretty poetry always did
make my eyes water
and can you believe it
all the women was cryin'
and though they was moanin'
other men's names
I just know they was cryin'
for me (poor critters)
and though I'd slept with all a them,
I'd forgotten
in all the big excitement
to tell 'em my name

and all the men looked angry
but I guess it was because the kids
was all being impolite
and a throwin' tin cans at me,
but I told 'em not to worry
because their aim was bad anyhow
not a boy there looked like he'd turn
into a man—
90% homosexuals, the lot of them,
and some guy shouted
"let's send him to hell!"

and with a jerk I was dancin'
my last dance,
but I swung out wide
and spit in the bartender's eye
and stared down
into Nellie Adam's breasts,
and my mouth watered again.

Scarlet

I'm glad when they arrive
and I'm glad when they leave

I'm glad when I hear their heels
approaching my door
and I'm glad when those heels
walk away

I'm glad to fuck
I'm glad to care
and I'm glad when it's over

and
since it's always either
starting or finishing
I'm glad
most of the time

and the cats walk up and down
and the earth spins around the sun
and the phone rings:

"this is Scarlet."

"who?"

"Scarlet."

"o.k., get it on over."

and I hang up thinking
maybe this is it

go in
take a quick shit
shave

bathe

dress

dump the sacks
and cartons of empty
bottles

sit down to the sound of
heels approaching
more an army approaching than
victory

it's Scarlet
and in my kitchen the faucet
keeps dripping
needs a washer.

I'll take care of it
later.

like a flower in the rain

I cut the middle fingernail of the middle
finger
right hand
real short
and I began rubbing along her cunt
as she sat upright in bed
spreading lotion over her arms
face
and breasts
after bathing.
then she lit a cigarette:
"don't let this put you off,"
and smoked and continued to rub the
lotion on.
I continued to rub the cunt.
"you want an apple?" I asked.
"sure," she said, "you got one?"
but I got to her—
she began to twist
then she rolled on her side,
she was getting wet and open
like a flower in the rain.
then she rolled on her stomach
and her most beautiful ass
looked up at me
and I reached under and got the
cunt again.
she reached around and got my
cock, she rolled and twisted,
I mounted
my face falling into the mass
of red hair that overflowed

from her head
and my fattened cock entered
into the miracle.

later we joked about the lotion
and the cigarette and the apple.
then I went out and got some chicken
and shrimp and french fries and buns
and mashed potatoes and gravy and
cole slaw, and we ate. she told me
how good she felt and I told her
how good I felt and we ate
the chicken and the shrimp and the
french fries and the buns and the
mashed potatoes and the gravy and
the cole slaw too.

a killer

consistency is terrific:
shark-mouth
grubby interior with an
almost perfect body,
long blazing hair—
it confuses me
and others

she runs from man to man
offering endearments

she speaks of love

then breaks each man
to her will

shark-mouthed
grubby interior

we see it too late:
after the cock gets swallowed
the heart follows

her long blazing hair
her almost perfect body
walks down the street
as the same sun
falls upon flowers.

prayer in bad weather

by God, I don't know what to
do.
they're so nice to have around.
they have a way of playing with
the balls
and looking at the cock very
seriously
turning it
tweeking it
examining each part
as their long hair falls on
your belly.

it's not the fucking and sucking
alone that reaches into a man
and softens him, it's the extras,
it's all the extras.

now it's raining tonight
and there's nobody
they are elsewhere
examining things
in new bedrooms
in new moods
or maybe in old
bedrooms.

anyhow, it's raining tonight,
one hell of a dashing, pouring
rain. . . .

very little to do.
I've read the newspaper
paid the gas bill
the electric co.
the phone bill.

it keeps raining.

they soften a man
and then let him swim
in his own juice.

I need an old-fashioned whore
at the door tonight
closing her green umbrella,
drops of moonlit rain on her
purse, saying, "shit, man,
can't you get better music
than *that* on your radio?
and turn up the heat . . ."

it's always when a man's swollen
with love and everything
else
that it keeps raining
splattering
flooding
rain
good for the trees and the
grass and the air . . .
good for things that
live alone.

I would give anything
for a female's hand on me
tonight.
they soften a man and
then leave him
listening to the rain.

melancholia

the history of melancholia
includes all of us.

me, I writhe in dirty sheets
while staring at blue walls
and nothing.

I have gotten so used to melancholia
that
I greet it like an old
friend.

I will now do 15 minutes of grieving
for the lost redhead,
I tell the gods.

I do it and feel quite bad
quite sad,
then I rise
CLEANSED
even though nothing is
solved.

that's what I get for kicking
religion in the ass.

I should have kicked the redhead
in the ass
where her brains and her bread and
butter are
at . . .

but, no, I've felt sad
about everything:
the lost redhead was just another
smash in a lifelong
loss . . .

I listen to drums on the radio now
and grin.

there is something wrong with me
besides
melancholia.

eat your heart out

I've come by, she says, to tell you
that this is it. I'm not kidding, it's
over. this is it.

I sit on the couch watching her arrange
her long red hair before my bedroom
mirror.
she pulls her hair up and
piles it on top of her head—
she lets her eyes look at
my eyes—
then she drops the hair and
lets it fall down in front of her face.

we go to bed and I hold her
speechlessly from the back
my arm around her neck
I touch her wrists and hands
feel up to
her elbows
no further.

she gets up.

this is it, she says,
eat your heart out. you
got any rubber bands?

I don't know.

here's one, she says,
this will do. well,
I'm going.

I get up and walk her
to the door

just as she leaves
she says,
I want you to buy me
some high-heeled shoes
with tall thin spikes,
black high-heeled shoes.
no, I want them
red.

I watch her walk down the cement walk
under the trees
she walks all right and
as the poinsettias drip in the sun
I close the door.

I made a mistake

I reached up into the top of the closet
and took out a pair of blue panties
and showed them to her and
asked "are these yours?"

and she looked and said,
"no, those belong to a dog."

she left after that and I haven't seen
her since. she's not at her place.
I keep going there, leaving notes stuck
into the door. I go back and the notes
are still there. I take the Maltese cross
cut it down from my car mirror, tie it
to her doorknob with a shoelace, leave
a book of poems.
when I go back the next night everything
is still there.

I keep searching the streets for that
blood-wine battleship she drives
with a weak battery, and the doors
hanging from broken hinges.

I drive around the streets
an inch away from weeping,
ashamed of my sentimentality and
possible love.

a confused old man driving in the rain
wondering where the good luck
went.

she comes from somewhere

probably from the belly button or from the shoe under the
bed, or maybe from the mouth of the shark or from
the car crash on the avenue that leaves blood and memories
scattered on the grass.
she comes from love gone wrong under an
asphalt moon.
she comes from screams stuffed with cotton.
she comes from hands without arms
and arms without bodies
and bodies without hearts.
she comes out of cannons and shotguns and old victrolas.
she comes from parasites with blue eyes and soft voices.
she comes out from under the organ like a roach.
she keeps coming.
she's inside of sardine cans and letters.
she's under your fingernails pressing blue and flat.
she's the signpost on the barricade
smeared in brown.
she's the toy soldiers inside your head
poking their lead bayonets.
she's the first kiss and the last kiss and
the dog's guts spilling like a river.
she comes from somewhere and she never stops
coming.

me, and that
old woman:
sorrow.

The High-Rise of the New World

it is an orange
animal
with
hand grenades
fire power
big teeth and
a horn of smoke

a colored man
with cigar
yanks at
gears and the damn thing never gets
tired

my neighbor
. . . an old man in blue
bathing trunks
. . . an old man
a fetid white obscene
thing—
the old man
lifts apart some purple flowers
and peeks through the fence at the
orange animal

and like a horror movie
I see the orange animal open its
mouth—
it belches it has teeth fastened onto a giraffe's
neck—
and it reached over the fence and it gets the
old man in his blue

bathing trunks
neatly
it gets him
from behind the fence of purple flowers
and his whiteness is like
garbage in the air
and then
he's dumped into a
shock of lumber

and then the orange animal
backs off
spins
turns
runs off into the Hollywood Hills
the palm trees the
boulevards as

the colored man
sucks red steam
from his
cigar

I'll be glad when it's all
over
the noise is
terrible and I'm afraid to go and
buy a
paper.

car wash

got out, fellow said, "hey!" walked toward
me, we shook hands, he slipped me 2 red
tickets for free car washes, "find you later,"
I told him, walked on through to waiting
area with wife, we sat on outside bench.
black fellow with a limp came up, said,
"hey, man, how's it going?"
I answered, "fine, bro, you makin' it?"
"no problem," he said, then walked off to
dry down a Caddy.
"these people know you?" my wife asked.
"no."
"how come they talk to you?"
"they like me, people have always liked me,
it's my cross."
then our car was finished, fellow flipped
his rag at me, we got up, got to the
car, I slipped him a buck, we got in, I
started the engine, the foreman walked
up, big guy with dark shades, huge guy,
he smiled a big one, "good to see you,
man!"
I smiled back, "thanks, but it's your party,
man!"
I pulled out into traffic, "they know you,"
said my wife.
"sure," I said, "I've been there."

Van Gogh

vain vanilla ladies strutting
while van Gogh did it to
himself.

girls pulling on silk
hose
while van Gogh did it to
himself
in the field

unkissed, and
worse.

I pass him on the street:
"how's it going, Van?"

"I dunno, man," he says
and walks on.

there is a blast of color:
one more creature
dizzy with love.

he said,
then,
I want to leave.

and they look at his paintings
and love him
now.

for that kind of love
he did the right
thing

as for the other kind of love
it never arrived.

the railroad yard

the feelings I get
driving past the railroad yard
(never on purpose but on my way to somewhere)
are the feelings other men have for other things.
I see the tracks and all the boxcars
the tank cars the flat cars
all of them motionless and so many of them
perfectly lined up and not an engine anywhere
(where are all the engines?).
I drive past looking sideways at it all
a wide, still railroad yard
not a human in sight
then I am past the yard
and it wasn't just the romance of it all
that gives me what I get
but something back there nameless
always making me feel better
as some men feel better looking at the open sea
or the mountains or at wild animals
or at a woman
I like those things too
especially the wild animals and the woman
but when I see those lovely old boxcars
with their faded painted lettering
and those flat cars and those fat round tankers
all lined up and waiting
I get quiet inside
I get what other men get from other things
I just feel better and it's good to feel better
whenever you can
not needing a reason.

the girls at the green
hotel

are more beautiful than
movie stars
and they lounge on the
lawn
sunbathing
and one sits in a short
dress and high
heels, legs crossed
exposing miraculous
thighs.
she has a bandanna
on her head
and smokes a
long cigarette.
traffic slows
almost stops.

the girls ignore
the traffic.
they are half
asleep in the afternoon
they are whores
they are whores without
souls
and they are magic
because they lie
about nothing.

I get in my car
wait for traffic to
clear,

drive across the street
to the green hotel
to my favorite:
she is
sunbathing on the
lawn nearest the
curb.

"hello," I say.
she turns eyes like
imitation diamonds
up at me.
her face has no
expression.

I drop my latest
book of poems
out the car
window.
it falls
by her side.

I shift into
low,
drive off.

there'll be some
laughs
tonight.

in other words

the Egyptians loved the cat
were often entombed with it
instead of with the women
and never with the dog

but now
here
good people with
good eyes
are very few

yet fine cats
with great style
lounge about
in the alleys of
the universe.

about
our argument tonight
whatever it was
about
and
no matter
how unhappy
it made us
feel

remember that
there is a
cat
somewhere
adjusting to the

space of itself
with a delightful
grace

in other words
magic persists
without us
no matter what
we may try to do
to spoil it.

Destroying Beauty

a rose
red sunlight;
I take it apart
in the garage
like a puzzle:
the petals are as greasy
as old bacon
and fall
like the maidens of the world
backs to floor
and I look up
at the old calendar
hung from a nail
and touch
my wrinkled face
and smile
because
the secret
is beyond me.

peace

near the corner table in the
cafe
a middle-aged couple
sit.
they have finished their
meal
and they are each drinking a
beer.
it is 9 in the evening.
she is smoking a
cigarette.
then he says something.
she nods.
then she speaks.
he grins, moves his
hand.
then they are
quiet.
through the blinds next to
their table
flashing red neon
blinks on and
off.

there is no war.
there is no hell.

then he raises his beer
bottle.
it is green.
he lifts it to his lips,
tilts it.

it is a coronet.

her right elbow is
on the table
and in her hand
she holds the
cigarette
between her thumb and
forefinger
and
as she watches
him
the streets outside
flower
in the
night.

afternoons into night

looking out the window
smoking rolled cigarettes
drinking Sanka
and watching the workers
come on in
I wonder, how much longer
can I get away with this?
stories and poems and
paintings
surviving on that.

an insane girlfriend
years younger
who loves me
types at her novel
in the kitchen.

my stories, my poems . . .
what is a poem?

a book by Céline sits on
the edge of the bathtub.
I read it when I bathe
and laugh.

the workers come in now
I see their faces,
the insides scraped away,
the outsides
missing.
I've had their jobs,

their goldfish
security.

Segovia plays to me
so softly from the
radio, the daylight's going.
look here—
the trip's been worth it,
while the jetliners go to New York and
Georgia and Texas
I sit surrounded by hymns that
nobody can ever take away
as the workers bend over
hot soup and cold
wives.

(uncollected)

we ain't got no money, honey, but we got rain

call it the greenhouse effect or whatever
but it just doesn't rain like it
used to.

I particularly remember the rains of the
depression era.
there wasn't any money but there was
plenty of rain.

it wouldn't rain for just a night or
a day,
it would RAIN for 7 days and 7
nights
and in Los Angeles the storm drains
weren't built to carry off that much
water
and the rain came down THICK and
MEAN and
STEADY
and you HEARD it banging against
the roofs and into the ground
waterfalls of it came down
from the roofs
and often there was HAIL
big ROCKS OF ICE
bombing
exploding
smashing into things
and the rain
just wouldn't
STOP
and all the roofs leaked—

361

dishpans,
cooking pots
were placed all about;
they dripped loudly
and had to be emptied
again and
again.

the rain came up over the street curbings,
across the lawns, climbed the steps and
entered the houses.
there were mops and bathroom towels,
and the rain often came up through the
toilets: bubbling, brown, crazy, whirling,
and the old cars stood in the streets,
cars that had problems starting on a
sunny day,
and the jobless men stood
looking out the windows
at the old machines dying
like living things
out there.

the jobless men,
failures in a failing time
were imprisoned in their houses with their
wives and children
and their
pets.
the pets refused to go out
and left their waste in
strange places.

the jobless men went mad
confined with
their once beautiful wives.
there were terrible arguments
as notices of foreclosure
fell into the mailbox.
rain and hail, cans of beans,
bread without butter; fried
eggs, boiled eggs, poached
eggs; peanut butter
sandwiches, and an invisible
chicken
in every pot.

my father, never a good man
at best, beat my mother
when it rained
as I threw myself
between them,
the legs, the knees, the
screams
until they
separated.

"*I'll kill you,*" I screamed
at him. "*You hit her again
and I'll kill you!*"

"*Get that son-of-a-bitching
kid out of here!*"

"no, Henry, you stay with
your mother!"

all the households were under
siege but I believe that ours
held more terror than the
average.

and at night
as we attempted to sleep
the rains still came down
and it was in bed
in the dark
watching the moon against
the scarred window
so bravely
holding out
most of the rain,
I thought of Noah and the
Ark
and I thought, it has come
again.
we all thought
that.

and then, at once, it would
stop.
and it always seemed to
stop
around 5 or 6 a.m.,
peaceful then,
but not an exact silence

because things continued to
drip
    drip
        drip

and there was no smog then
and by 8 a.m.
there was a
blazing yellow sunlight,
van Gogh yellow—
crazy, blinding!
and then
the roof drains
relieved of the rush of
water
began to expand in
the warmth:
PANG! PANG! PANG!

and everybody got up
and looked outside
and there were all the lawns
still soaked
greener than green will ever
be
and there were the birds
on the lawn
CHIRPING like mad,
they hadn't eaten decently
for 7 days and 7 nights
and they were weary of
berries

and
they waited as the worms
rose to the top,
half-drowned worms.
the birds plucked them
up
and gobbled them
down; there were
blackbirds and sparrows.
the blackbirds tried to
drive the sparrows off
but the sparrows,
maddened with hunger,
smaller and quicker,
got their
due.

the men stood on their porches
smoking cigarettes,
now knowing
they'd have to go out
there
to look for that job
that probably wasn't
there, to start that car
that probably wouldn't
start.

and the once beautiful
wives
stood in their bathrooms
combing their hair,

applying makeup,
trying to put their world back
together again,
trying to forget that
awful sadness that
gripped them,
wondering what they could
fix for
breakfast.

and on the radio
we were told that
school was now
open.
and
soon
there I was
on the way to school,
massive puddles in the
street,
the sun like a new
world,
my parents back in that
house,
I arrived at my classroom
on time.

Mrs. Sorenson greeted us
with, "we won't have our
usual recess, the grounds
are too wet."

"AW!" most of the boys
went.

"but we are going to do
something special at
recess," she went on,
"and it will be
fun!"

well, we all wondered
what that would
be
and the two-hour wait
seemed a long time
as Mrs. Sorenson
went about
teaching her
lessons.

I looked at the little
girls, they all looked so
pretty and clean and
alert,
they sat still and
straight
and their hair was
beautiful
in the California
sunshine.

then the recess bell rang
and we all waited for the
fun.

then Mrs. Sorenson told
us:
"now, what we are going to
do is we are going to tell
each other what we did
during the rainstorm!
we'll begin in the front
row and go right around!
now, Michael, you're
first! . . ."

well, we all began to tell
our stories, Michael began
and it went on and on,
and soon we realized that
we were all lying, not
exactly lying but mostly
lying and some of the boys
began to snicker and some
of the girls began to give
them dirty looks and
Mrs. Sorenson said,
"all right, I demand a
modicum of silence
here!
I am interested in what
you did
during the rainstorm

even if you
aren't!"

so we had to tell our
stories and they *were*
stories.

one girl said that
when the rainbow first
came
she saw God's face
at the end of it.
only she didn't say
which end.

one boy said he stuck
his fishing pole
out the window
and caught a little
fish
and fed it to his
cat.

almost everybody told
a lie.
the truth was just
too awful and
embarrassing to
tell.

then the bell rang
and recess was
over.

"thank you," said Mrs.
Sorenson, "that was very
nice.
and tomorrow the grounds
will be dry
and we will put them
to use
again."

most of the boys
cheered
and the little girls
sat very straight and
still,
looking so pretty and
clean and
alert,
their hair beautiful
in a sunshine that
the world might
never see
again.

marina:

majestic, magic
infinite
my little girl is
sun
on the carpet—
out the door
picking a
flower, ha!,
an old man,
battle-wrecked,
emerges from his
chair
and she looks at me
but only sees
love,
ha!, and I become
quick with the world
and love right back
just like I was meant
to do.

Trollius and trellises

of course, I may die in the next ten minutes
and I'm ready for that
but what I'm really worried about is
that my editor-publisher might retire
even though he is ten years younger than
I.
it was just 25 years ago (I was at that *ripe*
old age of 45)
when we began our unholy alliance to
test the literary waters,
neither of us being much
known.

I think we had some luck and still have some
of same
yet
the odds are pretty fair
that he will opt for warm and pleasant
afternoons
in the garden
long before I.

writing is its own intoxication
while publishing and editing,
attempting to collect bills
carries its own
attrition
which also includes dealing with the
petty bitchings and demands
of many
so-called genius darlings who are
not.

I won't blame him for getting
out
and hope he sends me photos of his
Rose Lane, his
Gardenia Avenue.

will I have to seek other
promulgators?
that fellow in the Russian
fur hat?
or that beast in the East
with all that hair
in his ears, with those wet and
greasy lips?

or will my editor-publisher
upon exiting for that world of Trollius and
trellis
hand over the
machinery
of his former trade to a
cousin, a
daughter or
some Poundian from Big
Sur?

or will he just pass the legacy on
to the
Shipping Clerk
who will rise like
Lazarus,

fingering newfound
importance?

one can imagine terrible
things:
"Mr. Chinaski, all your work
must now be submitted in
Rondo form
and
typed
triple-spaced on rice
paper."

power corrupts,
life aborts
and all you
have left
is a
bunch of
warts.

"no, no, Mr. Chinaski:
Rondo form!"

"hey, man," I'll ask,
"haven't you heard of
the thirties?"

"the thirties? what's
that?"

my present editor-publisher
and I
at times
did discuss the thirties,
the Depression
and
some of the little tricks it
taught us—
like how to endure on almost
nothing
and move forward
anyhow.

well, John, if it happens enjoy your
divertissement to
plant husbandry,
cultivate and aerate
between
bushes, water only in the
early morning, spread
shredding to discourage
weed growth
and
as I do in my writing:
use plenty of
manure.

and thank you
for locating me there at
5124 DeLongpre Avenue
somewhere between

alcoholism and
madness.

together we
laid down the gauntlet
and there are takers
even at this late date
still to be
found
as the fire sings
through the
trees.

beagle

do not bother the beagle lying there
away from grass and flowers and paths,
dreaming dogdreams, or perhaps dreaming
nothing, as men do awake;
yes, leave him be, in that simple juxtaposition,
out of the maelstrom, lucifugous as a bat,
searching bat-inward
for a state of grace.

it's good. we'll not ransom our fate
or his for doorknobs or rasps.
the east wind whirls the blinds,
our beagle snuffles in his sleep as
outside, outside,
hedges break, the night torn mad
with footsteps.

our beagle spreads a paw,
the lamp burns warm
bathed in the life of his
size.

coffee and babies

I sleep at Lila's and in the morning
we get the breakfast special at the local cafe,
then it's up to her friend Buffy's.
Buffy has boy twins, father in doubt, and lives on relief
in a $150-a-month apt.
the twins wail, crawl about, I pick one up, he pulls at
my goatee.
"how nice," I say, "to be sitting with 2 lovely ladies
at ten in the morning in the city of Burbank while
other men work."

every time the twins get changed I note they have hard-ons
(their troubles begin at the age of one)
and their asses are red with rash and sadness.
"I used to open and close the bars," I say,
"I used to whip men 20 years younger than myself. now I sit
with women and babies."

we have our coffees. I borrow a cigarette. (Buffy knows I
am good for it. I'll buy her a pack
later.) the girls joke about my ugly face.
I smoke. after this I need some profundities but
Buddha doesn't help much.
Buffy gets up and shakes her behind at me:
"you can't have me, Chinaski, you're too old, you're too
ugly."
well, you see, it's difficult for me. Lila and I finish
our coffees and climb down the green steps to the
blue-green
swimming pool. it is 11 a.m. India and Pakistan are at
war. we get into my smashed '62 Comet. it
starts. well, we can go to the races, we can screw again,

we can sleep, we can have a Mexican marriage, we can argue
and split or she can read to me about fresh murders in the
Herald-Examiner.
it ends up
we argue and split and I forget to go get
Buffy her pack of
cigarettes.

(uncollected)

magical mystery tour

I am in this low-slung sports car
painted a deep, rich yellow
driving under an Italian sun.
I have a British accent.
I'm wearing dark shades
an expensive silk shirt.
there's no dirt under my
fingernails.
the radio plays Vivaldi
and there are two women with
me
one with raven hair
the other a blonde.
they have small breasts and
beautiful legs
and they laugh at everything I
say.

as we drive up a steep road
the blonde squeezes my leg
and nestles closer
while raven hair
leans across and nibbles my
ear.

we stop for lunch at a quaint
rustic inn.
there is more laughter
before lunch
during lunch and after
lunch.

after lunch we will have a
flat tire on the other side of
the mountain
and the blonde will change the
tire
while
raven hair
photographs me
lighting my pipe
leaning against a tree
the perfect background
perfectly at peace
with
sunlight
flowers
clouds
birds
everywhere.

(uncollected)

the last generation

it was much easier to be a genius in the twenties, there were
only 3 or 4 literary magazines and if you got into them
4 or 5 times you could end up in Gertie's parlor
you could possibly meet Picasso for a glass of wine, or
maybe only Miró.

and yes, if you sent your stuff postmarked from Paris
chances of publication became much better.
most writers bottomed their manuscripts with the
word "Paris" and the date.

and with a patron there was time to
write, eat, drink and take drives to Italy and sometimes
Greece.
it was good to be photo'd with others of your kind
it was good to look tidy, enigmatic and thin.
photos taken on the beach were great.

and yes, you could write letters to the 15 or 20
others
bitching about this and that.

you might get a letter from Ezra or from Hem; Ezra liked
to give directions and Hem liked to practice his writing
in his letters when he couldn't do the other.

it was a romantic grand game then, full of the fury of
discovery.

now

now there are so many of us, hundreds of literary magazines,
hundreds of presses, thousands of titles.

who is to survive out of all this mulch?
it's almost improper to ask.

I go back, I read the books about the lives of the boys
and girls of the twenties.
if they were the Lost Generation, what would you call us?
sitting here among the warheads with our electric-touch
typewriters?

the Last Generation?

I'd rather be Lost than Last but as I read these books about
them
I feel a gentleness and a generosity

as I read of the suicide of Harry Crosby in his hotel room
with his whore
that seems as real to me as the faucet dripping now
in my bathroom sink.

I like to read about *them*: Joyce blind and prowling the
bookstores like a tarantula, they said.
Dos Passos with his clipped newscasts using a pink type-
writer ribbon.
D.H. horny and pissed off, H.D. being smart enough to use
her initials which seemed much more literary than Hilda
Doolittle.

G. B. Shaw, long established, as noble and
dumb as royalty, flesh and brain turning to marble. a
bore.

Huxley promenading his brain with great glee, arguing
with Lawrence that it wasn't in the belly and the balls,
that the glory was in the skull.

and that hick Sinclair Lewis coming to light.

meanwhile
the revolution being over, the Russians were liberated and
dying.
Gorky with nothing to fight for, sitting in a room trying
to find phrases praising the government.
many others broken in victory.

now

now there are so many of us
but we should be grateful, for in a hundred years
if the world is not destroyed, think, how much
there will be left of all of this:
nobody really able to fail or to succeed—just
relative merit, diminished further by
our numerical superiority.
we will all be catalogued and filed.
all right . . .

if you still have doubts of those other golden
times
there were other curious creatures: Richard

Aldington, Teddy Dreiser, F. Scott, Hart Crane, Wyndham
    Lewis, the
Black Sun Press.

but to me, the twenties centered mostly on Hemingway
coming out of the war and beginning to type.

it was all so simple, all so deliciously clear

now

there are so many of us.

Ernie, you had no idea how good it had been
four decades later when you blew your brains into
the orange juice

although
I grant you
that was not your best work.

about competition

the higher you climb
the greater the pressure.

those who manage to
endure
learn
that the distance
between the
top and the
bottom
is
obscenely
great.

and those who
succeed
know
this secret:
there isn't
one.

a radio with guts

it was on the 2nd floor on Coronado Street
I used to get drunk
and throw the radio through the window
while it was playing, and, of course,
it would break the glass in the window
and the radio would sit out there on the roof
still playing
and I'd tell my woman,
"Ah, what a marvelous radio!"

the next morning I'd take the window
off the hinges
and carry it down the street
to the glass man
who would put in another pane.

I kept throwing that radio through the window
each time I got drunk
and it would sit out there on the roof
still playing—
a magic radio
a radio with guts,
and each morning I'd take the window
back to the glass man.

I don't remember how it ended exactly
though I do remember
we finally moved out.
there was a woman downstairs who worked in
the garden in her bathing suit
and her husband complained he couldn't sleep nights
because of me

so we moved out
and in the next place
I either forgot to throw the radio out the window
or I didn't feel like it
anymore.

I do remember missing the woman who worked in the
garden in her bathing suit,
she really dug with that trowel
and she put her behind up in the air
and I used to sit in the window
and watch the sun shine all over that thing

while the music played.

the egg

he's 17.
mother, he said, how do I crack an
egg?

all right, she said to me, you don't have to
sit there looking like that.

oh, mother, he said, you broke the yolk.
I can't eat a broken yolk.

all right, she said to me, you're so tough,
you've been in the slaughterhouses, factories,
the jails, you're so goddamned tough,
but all people don't have to be like you,
that doesn't make everybody else wrong and you
right.

mother, he said, can you bring me some cokes
when you come home from work?

look, Raleigh, she said, can't you get the cokes
on your bike, I'm tired after
work.

but, mama, there's a hill.

what hill, Raleigh?

there's a hill,
it's there and I have to pedal over
it.

all right, she said to me, you think you're so
goddamned tough. you worked on a railroad track
gang, I hear about it every time you get drunk:
"I worked on a railroad track gang."

well, I said, I did.

I mean, what difference does it make?
everybody has to work somewhere.

mama, said the kid, will you bring me those
cokes?

I really like the kid. I think he's very
gentle. and once he learns how to crack an
egg he may do some
unusual things. meanwhile
I sleep with his mother
and try to stay out of
arguments.

a killer gets ready

he was a good one
say 18, 19,
a marine
and every time
a woman came down the train aisle
he seemed to stand up
so I couldn't see
her
and the woman smiled at him

but I didn't smile
at him

he kept looking at himself in the
train window
and standing up and taking off his
coat and then standing up
and putting it back
on

he polished his belt buckle with a
delighted vigor

and his neck was red and
his face was red and his eyes were a
pretty blue

but I didn't like
him

and every time I went to the can
he was either in one of the cans

or he was in front of one of the mirrors
combing his hair or
shaving

and he was always walking up and down the
aisles
or drinking water
I watched his Adam's apple juggle the water
down

he was always in my
eyes

but we never spoke
and I remembered all the other trains
all the other buses
all the other wars

he got off at Pasadena
vainer than any woman
he got off at Pasadena
proud and
dead

the rest of the train ride—
8 or 10 miles—
was perfect.

in the center of the action

you have to lay down like an animal
until it
charges, you
have to lay down
in the center of the action

lay down and wait until it charges then you
must get
up
face it get
it before it gets
you

the whole process is more
shy than
vulnerable so

lay down and wait sometimes it's
ten minutes sometimes it's years sometimes it
never arrives but you can't rush it push
it
there's no way to cheat or get a
jump on it you have to

lay down
lay down and wait like
an animal.

poetry

it
takes
a lot of

desperation

dissatisfaction

and
disillusion

to
write

a
few
good
poems.

it's not
for
everybody

either to

write
it

or even to

read
it.

notes upon the flaxen aspect:

a John F. Kennedy flower knocks upon my door and is
shot through the neck;
the gladiolas gather by the dozens around the tip of
India
dripping into Ceylon;
dozens of oysters read Germaine Greer.

meanwhile, I itch from the slush of the Philippines
to the eye of the minnow
the minnow being eaten by the cumulative dreams of
Simón Bolívar. O,
freedom from the limitation of angular distance would be
delicious.
war is perfect,
the solid way drips and leaks,
Schopenhauer laughed for 72 years,
and I was told by a very small man in a New York City
pawnshop
one afternoon:
"Christ got more attention than I did
but I went further on less . . ."

well, the distance between 5 points is the same as the
distance between 3 points is the same as the distance
between one point:

it is all as cordial as a bonbon:
all this that we are wrapped
in:

eunuchs are more exact than sleep

the postage stamp is mad, Indiana is ridiculous

the chameleon is the last walking flower.

the fisherman

he comes out at 7:30 a.m. every day
with 3 peanut butter sandwiches, and
there's one can of beer
which he floats in the bait bucket.
he fishes for hours with a small trout pole
three-quarters of the way down the pier.
he's 75 years old and the sun doesn't tan him,
and no matter how hot it gets
the brown and green lumberjack stays on.
he catches starfish, baby sharks, and mackerel;
he catches them by the dozen,
speaks to nobody.
sometime during the day
he drinks his can of beer.
at 6 p.m. he gathers his gear and his catch
walks down the pier
across several streets
where he enters a small Santa Monica apartment
goes to the bedroom and opens the evening paper
as his wife throws the starfish, the sharks, the mackerel
into the garbage

he lights his pipe
and waits for dinner.

the 1930s

places to hunt
places to hide are
getting harder to find, and pet
canaries and goldfish too, did you notice
that?
I remember when pool halls were pool halls
not just tables in
bars;
and I remember when neighborhood women
used to cook pots of beef stew for their
unemployed husbands
when their bellies were sick with
fear;
and I remember when kids used to watch the rain
for hours and
would fight to the end over a pet
rat; and
I remember when the boxers were all Jewish and Irish
and never gave you a
bad fight; and when the biplanes flew so low you
could see the pilot's face and goggles;
and when one ice cream bar in ten had a free coupon in-
side; and when for 3 cents you could buy enough candy
to make you sick
or last a whole
afternoon; and when the people in the neighborhood raised
chickens in their backyards; and when we'd stuff a 5-cent
toy auto full of
candle wax to make it last
forever; and when we built our own kites and scooters;
and I remember
when our parents fought

(you could hear them for blocks)
and they fought for hours, screaming blood-death curses
and the cops never
came.

places to hunt and places to hide,
they're just not around
anymore. I remember when
each 4th lot was vacant and overgrown, and the landlord
only got his rent
when you had
it, and each day was clear and good and each moment was
full of promise.

the burning of the dream

the old L.A. Public Library burned
down
that library downtown
and with it went
a large part of my
youth.

I sat on one of those stone
benches there with my friend
Baldy when he
asked,
"you gonna join the
Abraham Lincoln
Brigade?"

"sure," I told
him.

but realizing that I wasn't
an intellectual or a political
idealist
I backed off on that
one
later.

I was a *reader*
then
going from room to
room: literature, philosophy,
religion, even medicine
and geology.

early on
I decided to be a writer,
I thought it might be the easy
way
out
and the big boy novelists didn't look
too tough to
me.
I had more trouble with
Hegel and Kant.

the thing that bothered
me
about everybody
is that they took so long
to finally say
something lively and /
or
interesting.
I thought I had it
over everybody
then.

I was to discover two
things:
a) most publishers thought that anything
boring had something to do with things
profound.
b) that it would take decades of
living and writing
before I would be able to
put down

a sentence that was
anywhere near
what I wanted it to
be.

meanwhile
while other young men chased the
ladies
I chased the old
books.
I was a bibliophile, albeit a
disenchanted
one
and this
and the world
shaped me.

I lived in a plywood hut
behind a rooming house
for $3.50 a
week
feeling like a
Chatterton
stuffed inside of some
Thomas
Wolfe.

my greatest problem was
stamps, envelopes, paper
and
wine,
with the world on the edge

of World War II.
I hadn't yet been
confused by the
female, I was a virgin
and I wrote from 3 to
5 short stories a week
and they all came
back
from *The New Yorker, Harper's,*
The Atlantic Monthly.
I had read where
Ford Madox Ford used to paper
his bathroom with his
rejection slips
but I didn't have a
bathroom so I stuck them
into a drawer
and when it got so stuffed with them
I could barely
open it
I took all the rejects out
and threw them
away along with the
stories.

still
the old L.A. Public Library remained
my home
and the home of many other
bums.
we discreetly used the
restrooms

and the only ones of
us
to be evicted were those
who fell asleep at the
library
tables—nobody snores like a
bum
unless it's somebody you're married
to.

well, I wasn't *quite* a
bum. *I* had a library card
and I checked books in and
out
large
stacks of them
always taking the
limit
allowed:
Aldous Huxley, D. H. Lawrence,
e. e. cummings, Conrad Aiken, Fyodor
Dos, Dos Passos, Turgenev, Gorky,
H.D., Freddie Nietzsche, Art
Schopenhauer,
Steinbeck,
Hemingway,
and so
forth . . .

I always expected the librarian
to say, "you have good taste, young
man . . ."

but the old fried and wasted
bitch didn't even know who she
was
let alone
me.

but those shelves held
tremendous grace: they allowed
me to discover
the early Chinese poets
like Tu Fu and Li
Po
who could say more in one
line than most could say in
thirty or
a hundred.
Sherwood Anderson must have
read
these
too.

I also carried the *Cantos*
in and out
and Ezra helped me
strengthen my arms if not
my brain.

that wondrous place
the L.A. Public Library
it was a home for a person who had had
a
home of

hell
BROOKS TOO BROAD FOR LEAPING
FAR FROM THE MADDING CROWD
POINT COUNTER POINT
THE HEART IS A LONELY HUNTER

James Thurber
John Fante
Rabelais
de Maupassant

some didn't work for
me: Shakespeare, G. B. Shaw,
Tolstoy, Robert Frost, F. Scott
Fitzgerald

Upton Sinclair worked better for
me
than Sinclair Lewis
and I considered Gogol and
Dreiser complete
fools

but such judgments come more
from a man's
forced manner of living than from
his reason.

the old L.A. Public
most probably kept me from
becoming a
suicide

a bank
robber
a
wife-
beater
a butcher or a
motorcycle policeman
and even though some of these
might be fine
it is
thanks
to my luck
and my way
that this library was
there when I was
young and looking to
hold on to
something
when there seemed very
little
about.

and when I opened the
newspaper
and read of the fire
which
destroyed the
library and most of
its contents

I said to my
wife: "I used to spend my

time
there . . ."

THE PRUSSIAN OFFICER
THE DARING YOUNG MAN ON THE FLYING TRAPEZE
TO HAVE AND HAVE NOT

YOU CAN'T GO HOME AGAIN.

sit and endure

well, first Mae West died
and then George Raft,
and Eddie G. Robinson's
been gone
a long time,
and Bogart and Gable
and Grable,
and Laurel and
Hardy
and the Marx Brothers,
all those Saturday
afternoons
at the movies
as a boy
are gone now
and I look
around this room
and it looks back at me
and then out through
the window.
time hangs helpless
from the doorknob
as a gold
paperweight
of an owl
looks up at me
(an old man now)
who must sit and endure
these many empty
Saturday
afternoons.

Goldfish

my goldfish stares with watery eyes
into the hemisphere of my sorrow;
upon the thinnest of threads
we hang together,
hang hang hang
in the hangman's noose;
I stare into his place and
he into mine . . .
he must have thoughts,
can you deny this?
he has eyes and hunger
and his love too
died in January; but he is
gold, really gold, and I am gray
and it is indecent to search him out,
indecent like the burning of peaches
or the rape of children,
and I turn and look elsewhere,
but I know that he is there behind me,
one gold goblet of blood,
one thing alone
hung between the reddest cloud
of purgatory
and apt. no. 303.

god, can it be
that we are the same?

finish

the hearse comes through the room filled with
the beheaded, the disappeared, the living
mad.
the flies are a glue of sticky paste
their wings will not
lift.
I watch an old woman beat her cat
with a broom.
the weather is unendurable
a dirty trick by
God.
the water has evaporated from the
toilet bowl
the telephone rings without
sound
the small limp arm petering against the
bell.
I see a boy on his
bicycle
the spokes collapse
the tires turn into
snakes and melt
away.
the newspaper is oven-hot
men murder each other in the streets
without reason.
the worst men have the best jobs
the best men have the worst jobs or are
unemployed or locked in
madhouses.
I have 4 cans of food left.
air-conditioned troops go from house to

house
from room to room
jailing, shooting, bayoneting
the people.
we have done this to ourselves, we
deserve this
we are like roses that have never bothered to
bloom when we should have bloomed and
it is as if
the sun has become disgusted with
waiting
it is as if the sun were a mind that has
given up on us.
I go out on the back porch
and look across the sea of dead plants
now thorns and sticks shivering in a
windless sky.
somehow I'm glad we're through
finished—
the works of Art
the wars
the decayed loves
the way we lived each day.
when the troops come up here
I don't care what they do for
we already killed ourselves
each day we got out of bed.
I go back into the kitchen
spill some hash from a soft
can, it is almost cooked
already
and I sit

eating, looking at my
fingernails.
the sweat comes down behind my
ears and I hear the
shooting in the streets and
I chew and wait
without wonder.

dreaming

I live alone in a small room
and read the newspapers
and sleep alone in the dark
dreaming of crowds.

(uncollected)

my special craving

what is it about lobsters and crabs?
those white-pink shells
that always make me hungry just
looking at them there
in the butcher's display case
tossed casually one upon the other
so kind and pink and waiting.
even alive they make me hungry.
I used to unload them from trucks
for the kitchen at the Biltmore Hotel,
and they looked dangerous
moving about in their slatted boxes
but still they made me
hungry. there is something about
crabs and lobsters
they *deserve* to be eaten,
they go so well with
french fries, french bread, radishes
and beer. they tell me that they boil them
alive, and this does
cause some minor sense of disturbance within
me, but outside of that
lobsters and crabs are one of the few things
that make the earth a happy place.
I suppose that this is my special
craving. when driving along the beachfront
and I see a sign,
LOBSTER HOUSE, my car turns in of its own
accord. (if a man can't allow himself a
few luxuries
he just isn't going to last very
long.) crabs, beer, lobsters,

an occasional lady,
2 or 3 days a week at the track,
my small daughter bringing me a bottle of beer
from the refrigerator while
grinning proudly,
there are some wonderful things in life,
(let each man find his own)
I say lighting my cigar,
thinking about Sunday night lobster dinner,
love love love
running wild,
it feels good sometimes just to be living
with something so nice
in store.

(uncollected)

A Love Poem

all the women
all their kisses the
different ways they love and
talk and need.

their ears they all have
ears and
throats and dresses
and shoes and
automobiles and ex-
husbands.

mostly
the women are very
warm they remind me of
buttered toast with the butter
melted
in.

there is a look in the
eye: they have been
taken they have been
fooled. I don't quite know what to
do for
them.

I am
a fair cook a good
listener
but I never learned to
dance—I was busy
then with larger things.

but I've enjoyed their different
beds
smoking cigarettes
staring at the
ceilings. I was neither vicious nor
unfair. only
a student.

I know they all have these
feet and barefoot they go across the floor as
I watch their bashful buttocks in the
dark. I know that they like me, some even
love me
but I love very
few.

some give me oranges and vitamin pills;
others talk quietly of
childhood and fathers and
landscapes; some are almost
crazy but none of them are without
meaning; some love
well, others not
so; the best at sex are not always the
best in other
ways; each has limits as I have
limits and we learn
each other
quickly.

all the women all the
women all the

bedrooms
the rugs the
photos the
curtains, it's
something like a church only
at times there's
laughter.

those ears those
arms those
elbows those eyes

looking, the fondness and
the wanting I have been
held I have been
held.

there was a rock-and-mud slide
on the Pacific Coast Highway and we had to take a
detour and they directed us up into the Malibu hills
and traffic was slow and it was hot, and then
we were lost.
but I spotted a hearse and said, "there's the
hearse, we'll follow it," and my woman said,
"that's not the hearse," and I said, "yes, that's the
hearse."

the hearse took a left and I followed
it as it went up
a narrow dirt road and then pulled over and I
thought, "he's lost too." there was a truck and a man
selling strawberries parked there
and I pulled over
and asked
where the church was and he gave me directions and
my woman told the strawberry man, "we'll buy some
strawberries on the way back." then I swung
onto the road and the hearse started up again
and we continued to drive along
until we reached that
church.

we were going
to the funeral of a great man
but
the crowd was very sparse: the
family, a couple of old screenwriter friends,
two or three others. we
spoke to the family and to the wife of the deceased

and then we went in and the service began and the
priest wasn't so good but one of the great man's
sons gave a fine eulogy, and then it was over
and we were outside again, in our car,
following the hearse again, back down the steep
road
passing the strawberry truck again and my
woman said, "let's not stop for strawberries,"
and as we continued to the graveyard, I thought,
Fante, you were one of the best writers ever
and this is one sad day.
finally we were at the graveside, the priest
said a few words and then it was over.
I walked up to the widow who sat very pale and
beautiful and quite alone on a folding metal chair.
"Hank," she said, "it's hard," and I tried in vain
to say something that might comfort her.

we walked away then, leaving her there, and
I felt terrible.

I got a friend to drive my girlfriend back to
town while I drove to the racetrack, made it
just in time for the first race, got my bet
down as the mutuel clerk looked at me in wonder and
said, "Jesus Christ, how come you're wearing a
necktie?"

the wine of forever

re-reading some of Fante's
The Wine of Youth
in bed
this mid-afternoon
my big cat
BEAKER
asleep beside
me.

the writing of some
men
is like a vast bridge
that carries you
over
the many things
that claw and tear.

Fante's pure and magic
emotions
hang on the simple
clean
line.

that this man died
one of the slowest and
most horrible deaths
that I ever witnessed or
heard
about . . .

the gods play no
favorites.

I put the book down
beside me.

book on one side,
cat on the
other . . .

John, meeting you,
even the way it
was was the event of my
life. I can't say
I would have died for
you, I couldn't have handled
it that well.

but it was good to see you
again
this
afternoon.

the pile-up

the 3 horse clipped the heels of
the 7, they both went down and
the 9 stumbled over them,
jocks rolling, horses' legs flung
skyward.
then the jocks were up, stunned
but all right
and I watched the horses
rising in the late afternoon,
it had not been a good day for
me
and I watched the horses rise,
please, I said inside, no broken
legs!
and the 9 was all right
and the 7
and the 3 also,
they were walking,
the horses didn't need the van,
the jocks didn't need the
ambulance.
what a beautiful day,
what a perfectly beautiful day,
what a wondrously lovely
day—
3 winners in a
single race.

my big night on the town

sitting on a 2nd-floor porch at 1:30 a.m.
while
looking out over the city.
it could be worse.

we needn't accomplish great things, we only
need to accomplish little things that make us feel
better or
not so bad.

of course, sometimes the fates will
not allow us to do
this.

then, we must outwit the fates.

we must be patient with the gods.
they like to have fun,
they like to play with us.
they like to test us.
they like to tell us that we are weak
and stupid, that we are
finished.

the gods need to be amused.
we are their toys.

as I sit on the porch a bird begins
to serenade me from a tree nearby in
the dark.

it is a mockingbird.
I am in love with mockingbirds.

I make bird sounds.
he waits.
then he makes them back.

he is so good that I laugh.

we are all so easily pleased,
all of us living things.

now a slight drizzle begins to
fall.
little chill drops fall on my
hot skin.

I am half asleep.
I sit in a folding chair with my
feet up on the railing
as the mockingbird begins
to repeat every bird song
he has heard that
day.

this is what we old guys do
for amusement
on Saturday
nights:
we laugh at the gods, we
settle old scores with

them,
we rejuvenate
as the lights of the city
blink below,
as the dark tree
holding the mockingbird
watches over us,
and as the world,
from here,
looks as good as it ever
will.

close encounters of another kind

are we going to the movies or not?
she asked him.

all right, he said, let's go.

I'm not going to put any panties on
so you can finger-fuck me in the
dark, she said.

should we get buttered popcorn?
he asked.

sure, she said.

leave your panties on,
he said.

what is it? she asked.

I just want to watch the movie,
he answered.

look, she said, I could go out on
the street, there are a hundred men
out there who'd be delighted to have
me.

all right, he said, go ahead out there.
I'll stay home and read the *National
Enquirer*.

you son of a bitch, she said, I am
trying to build a meaningful
relationship.

you can't build it with a hammer,
he said.

are we going to the movies or not?
she asked.

all right, he said, let's
go . . .

at the corner of Western and
Franklin he put on the blinker
to make his left turn
and a man in the on-coming lane
speeded up
as if to cut him off.

brakes grabbed. there wasn't a
crash but there almost was one.

he cursed at the man in the other
car. the man cursed back. the
man had another person in the car with
him. it was *his* wife.

they were going to the movies
too.

drying out

we buy the scandal sheets at the supermarket
get into bed and eat pretzels and read as outside
the church bells ring and the dogs bark
we turn on the tv and watch very bad movies
then she goes down and brings up ice cream
and we eat the ice cream and she says,
"tomorrow night is trash night."
then the cat jumps up on the bed
drops its tongue out and stands there
glistening cross-eyed

the phone rings and it is her mother and she
talks to her mother
she hands me the phone
I tell her mother that it's too bad it's freezing
back there
it's about 85 here and,
yes, I'm feeling well and
I hope you're feeling well too

I hand the phone back

she talks some more
then hangs up

"mother is a very brave woman," she tells me
I tell her that I'm sure her mother is

the cat is still standing there glistening
cross-eyed
I push it down onto the covers

"well," she says, "we've gone two nights without
drinking."

"good," I say, "but tomorrow night I'm going to
do it."

"ah, come on," she says

"you don't have to drink," I tell her, "just because
I do."

"like hell," she says

she flips the remote control switch until she comes to a
Japanese monster movie

"I think we've seen this one," I say

"you didn't see it with me," she says, "who did you
see it with?"

"you were laying with me, right here, when we saw it,"
I tell her

"I don't think I remember this one," she says

"you just keep watching," I tell her

we keep watching
I'm not so sure anymore
but it's a peaceful night as we watch this big thing
kick the shit out of half of Tokyo.

scene from 1940:

"I knew you were a bad-ass," he said.
"you sat in the back of Art class and
you never said anything.
then I saw you in that brutal fight
with the guy with the dirty yellow
hair.
I like guys like you, you're rare, you're
raw, you make your own rules!"

"get your fucking face out of mine!"
I told him.

"you see?" he said. "you see?"

he disgusted me.
I turned and walked off.

he had outwitted me:
praise was the only thing I couldn't
handle.

the area of pause

you have to have it or the walls will close
in.
you have to give everything up, throw it
away, everything away.
you have to look at what you look at
or think what you think
or do what you do
or
don't do
without considering personal
advantage
without accepting guidance.

people are worn away with
striving,
they hide in common
habits.
their concerns are herd
concerns.

few have the ability to stare
at an old shoe for
ten minutes
or to think of odd things
like who invented the
doorknob?

they become unalive
because they are unable to
pause
undo themselves
unkink

unsee
unlearn
roll clear.
listen to their untrue
laughter, then
walk
away.

I know you

you with long hair, legs crossed high, sitting at the end of
the bar, you like a butcher knife against my throat
as the nightingale sings elsewhere while laughter
mingles with the roach's hiss.
I know you as
the piano player in the restaurant who plays badly,
his mouth a tiny cesspool and his eyes little wet rolls of
toilet paper.
you rode behind me on my bicycle as I pumped toward Venice as
a boy, I knew you were there, even in that brisk wind I smelled
your
breath.
I knew you in the love bed as you whispered lies of passion while
your
nails dug me into you.
I saw you adored by crowds in Spain while pigtail boys with
swords
colored the sun for your glory.
I saw you complete the circle of friend, enemy, celebrity and
stranger as the fox ran through the sun carrying its heart in its
mouth.
those madmen I fought in the back alleys of bars were
you.
you, yes, heard Plato's last words.
not too many mornings ago I found my old cat in the yard,
dry tongue stuck out awry as if it had never belonged, eyes tangled,
eyelids soft yet, I lifted her, daylight shining upon my
fingers and her fur, my ignorant existence roaring against the

hedges and the flowers.
I know you, you wait while the fountains gush and the scales weigh,
you tiresome daughter-of-a-bitch, come on in, the door is open.

relentless as the tarantula

they're not going to let you
sit at a front table
at some cafe in Europe
in the mid-afternoon sun.
if you do, somebody's going to
drive by and
spray your guts with a
submachine gun.

they're not going to let you
feel good
for very long
anywhere.
the forces aren't going to
let you sit around
fucking off and
relaxing.
you've got to do it
their way.

the unhappy, the bitter and
the vengeful
need their
fix—which is
you or somebody
anybody
in agony, or
better yet
dead, dropped into some
hole.

as long as there are
human beings about
there is never going to be
any peace
for any individual
upon this earth (or
anywhere else
they might
escape to).

all you can do
is maybe grab
ten lucky minutes
here
or maybe an hour
there.

something
is working toward you
right now, and
I mean you
and nobody but
you.

the replacements

Jack London drinking his life away while
writing of strange and heroic men.
Eugene O'Neill drinking himself oblivious
while writing his dark and poetic
works.

now our moderns
lecture at universities
in tie and suit,
the little boys soberly studious,
the little girls with glazed eyes
looking
up,
the lawns so green, the books so dull,
the life so dying of
thirst.

to lean back into it

like in a chair the color of the sun
as you listen to lazy piano music
and the aircraft overhead are not
at war.
where the last drink is as good as
the first
and you realized that the promises
you made yourself were
kept.
that's plenty.
that last: about the promises:
what's not so good is that the few
friends you had are
dead and they seem
irreplaceable.
as for women, you didn't know enough
early enough
and you knew enough
too late.
and if more self-analysis is allowed: it's
nice that you turned out well-
honed,
that you arrived late
and remained generally
capable.
outside of that, not much to say
except you can leave without
regret.
until then, a bit more amusement,
a bit more endurance,

leaning back
into it.

like the dog who got across
the busy street:
not all of it was good
luck.

eating my senior citizen's dinner at the Sizzler

between 2 and 5 p.m. any day and any time on Sunday and
Wednesday, it's 20% off for
us old dogs approaching the sunset.
it's strange to be old and not feel
old
but I glance in the mirror
see some silver hair
concede that I'd look misplaced at a
rock concert.

I eat alone.
the other oldies are in groups,
a man and a woman
a woman and a woman
three old women
another man and a
woman.
it's 4:30 p.m. on a
Tuesday
and just 5 or 6 blocks north is
the cemetery
on a long sloping green hill,
a very modern place with
the markers
flat on the ground,
it's much more pleasant for
passing traffic.

a young waitress
moves among us
filling our cups

again with lovely
poisonous caffeine.
we thank her and
chew on,
some with our own
teeth.

we wouldn't lose much in a
nuclear explosion.

one good old boy talks
on and on
about what
he's not too
sure.

well, I finish my meal,
leave a tip.
I have the last table by the
exit door.
as I'm about to leave
I'm blocked by an old girl
in a walker
followed by another old girl
whose back is bent
like a bow.
their faces, their arms
their hands are like
parchment
as if they had already been
embalmed
but they leave quietly.

as I made ready to leave
again
I am blocked
this time by a huge
wheelchair
the back tilted low
it's almost like a bed,
a very expensive
mechanism,
an awesome and glorious
receptacle
the chrome glitters
and the thick tires are
air-inflated
and the lady in the chair and
the lady pushing it
look alike,
sisters no doubt,
one's lucky
gets to ride,
and they go by
again very *white*.

and then
I rise
make it to the door
into stunning sunlight
make it to the car
get in
roar the engine into
life
rip it into reverse

with a quick back turn of squealing
tires
I slam to a bouncing halt
rip the wheel right
feed the gas
go from first to second
spin into a gap of
traffic
am quickly into
3rd
4th
I am up to
50 mph in a flash
moving through
them.
who can turn the stream
of destiny?
I light a cigarette
punch on the radio
and a young girl
sings,
"put it where it hurts,
daddy, make me love
you . . ."

it's strange

it's strange when famous people die
whether they have fought the good fight or
the bad one.
it's strange when famous people die
whether we like them or not
they are like old buildings old streets
things and places that we are used to
which we accept simply because they're
there.
it's strange when famous people die
it's like the death of a father or
a pet cat or dog.
and it's strange when famous people are killed
or when they kill themselves.
the trouble with the famous is that they must
be replaced and they can never quite be
replaced, and that gives us this unique
sadness.
it's strange when famous people die
the sidewalks look different and our
children look different and our bedmates
and our curtains and our automobiles.
it's strange when famous people die:

we become troubled.

The Beast

Beowulf may have killed Grendel and
Grendel's mother
but he
couldn't kill this
one:
it moves around with broken back and
eyes of spittle
has cancer
sweeps with a broom
smiles and kills
germs germans gladiolas

it sits in the bathtub
with a piece of soap and
reads the newspaper about the
Bomb and Vietnam and the freeways
and it smiles and then
gets out naked
doesn't use a towel
goes outside
and rapes young girls
kills them and
throws them aside like
steakbone

it walks into a bedroom and watches
lovers fuck
it stops the clock at
1:30 a.m.
it turns a man into a rock while he
reads a book

the beast
spoils candy
causes mournful songs to be
created
makes birds stop
flying

it even killed Beowulf
the brave Beowulf who
had killed Grendel and Grendel's
mother

look
even the whores at the bar
think about it
drink too much and
almost
forget business.

woman on the street

her shoes themselves
would light my room
like many candles.

she walks like all things
shining on glass,
like all things
that make a difference.

she walks away.

lost in San Pedro

no way back to Barcelona.
the green soldiers have invaded the tombs.
madmen rule Spain
and during a heat wave in 1952 I buried my last concubine.

no way back to the Rock of Gibraltar.
the bones of the hands of my mother are so still.

stay still now, mother
stay still.

the horse tossed the jock
the horse fell
then got up
on only 3 legs—
the 4th bent nearly in two
and all the people anguished for the jock
but my heart ached for the horse
the horse
the horse
it was terrible
it was truly terrible.

I sometimes think about one or the other of my women.
I wonder what we were hoping for when we lived together
our minds shattered like the 4th leg of that horse.

remember when women wore dresses and high heels?
remember whenever a car door opened all the men turned to look?
it was a beautiful time and I'm glad I was there to see it.

no way back to Barcelona.

the world is less than a fishbone.

this place roars with the need for mercy.

there is this fat gold watch sitting here on my desk
sent to me by a German cop.
I wrote him a nice letter thanking him for it
but the police have killed more of my life than the crooks.

nothing to do but wait for the pulling of the shade.
I pull the shade.

my 3 male cats have had their balls clipped.
now they sit and look at me with eyes emptied
of all but killing.

Manx

have we gone wrong again?
we laugh less and less,
become more sadly sane.
all we want is
the absence of others.
even favorite classical music
has been heard too often and
all the good books have been
read . . .

there is a sliding
glass door
and there outside
a white Manx sits
with one crossed eye
his tongue sticks out the
corner of his mouth.
I lean over
and pull the door open
and he comes running in
front legs working
in one direction,
rear legs
in the other.

he circles the
room in a scurvy angle
to where I sit
claws up my legs
my chest
places front legs
like arms

on my shoulders
sticks his snout
against my nose
and looks at me as
best he can.
also befuddled,
I look back.

a better night now,
old boy,
a better time,
a better way now
stuck together
like this
here.

I am able
to smile again
as suddenly
the Manx
leaps away
scattering across the
rug sideways
chasing something now
that none of us
can see.

the history of a tough motherfucker

he came to the door one night wet thin beaten and
terrorized
a white cross-eyed tailless cat
I took him in and fed him and he stayed
grew to trust me until a friend drove up the driveway
and ran him over
I took what was left to a vet who said, "not much
chance . . . give him these pills . . . his backbone
is crushed, but it was crushed before and somehow
mended, if he lives he'll never walk, look at
these x-rays, he's been shot, look here, the pellets
are still there . . . also, he once had a tail, somebody
cut it off . . ."

I took the cat back, it was a hot summer, one of the
hottest in decades, I put him on the bathroom
floor, gave him water and pills, he wouldn't eat, he
wouldn't touch the water, I dipped my finger into it
and wet his mouth and I talked to him, I didn't go any-
where, I put in a lot of bathroom time and talked to
him and gently touched him and he looked back at
me with those pale blue crossed eyes and as the days went
by he made his first move
dragging himself forward by his front legs
(the rear ones wouldn't work)
he made it to the litter box
crawled over and in,
it was like the trumpet of possible victory
blowing in that bathroom and into the city, I
related to that cat—I'd had it bad, not that
bad but bad enough . . .

one morning he got up, stood up, fell back down and
just looked at me.

"you can make it," I said to him.

he kept trying, getting up and falling down, finally
he walked a few steps, he was like a drunk, the
rear legs just didn't want to do it and he fell again, rested,
then got up.

you know the rest: now he's better than ever, cross-eyed,
almost toothless, but the grace is back, and that look in
his eyes never left . . .

and now sometimes I'm interviewed, they want to hear about
life and literature and I get drunk and hold up my cross-eyed,
shot, runover de-tailed cat and I say, "look, look
at *this*!"

but they don't understand, they say something like, "you
say you've been influenced by Céline?"

"no," I hold the cat up, "by what happens, by
things like this, by this, by *this*!"

I shake the cat, hold him up in
the smoky and drunken light, he's relaxed he knows . . .

it's then that the interviews end
although I am proud sometimes when I see the pictures
later and there I am and there is the cat and we are photo-
graphed together.

he too knows it's bullshit but that somehow it all helps.

bad fix

old Butch, they fixed him
the girls don't look like much
anymore.

when Big Sam moved out
of the back
I inherited big Butch,
70 as cats go,
old,
fixed,
but still as big and
mean a cat as anybody
ever remembered
seeing.

he's damn near gnawed
off my hand
the hand that feeds him
a couple of
times
but I've forgiven him,
he's fixed
and there's something in
him
that doesn't like
it.

at night
I hear him mauling and
running other cats through
the brush.

Butch, he's still a magnificent
old cat,
fighting
even without it.

what a bastard he must have been
with it
when he was 19 or 20
walking slowly down
his path
and I look at him
now
still feel the courage
and the strength
in spite of man's smallness
in spite of man's scientific
skill
old Butch
retains
endures

peering at me with those
evil yellow eyes
out of that huge
undefeated
head.

one for the old boy

he was just a
cat
cross-eyed,
a dirty white
with pale blue eyes

I won't bore you with his
history
just to say
he had much bad luck
and was a good old
guy
and he died
like people die
like elephants die
like rats die
like flowers die
like water evaporates and
the wind stops blowing

the lungs gave out
last Monday.
now he's in the rose
garden
and I've heard a
stirring march
playing for him
inside of me
which I know
not many
but some of you
would like to

know
about.

that's
all.

my cats

I know. I know.
they are limited, have different
needs and
concerns.

but I watch and learn from them.
I like the little they know,
which is so
much.

they complain but never
worry.
they walk with a surprising dignity.
they sleep with a direct simplicity that
humans just can't
understand.

their eyes are more
beautiful than our eyes.
and they can sleep 20 hours
a day
without
hesitation or
remorse.

when I am feeling
low
all I have to do is
watch my cats
and my
courage
returns.

I study these
creatures.

they are my
teachers.

Death Wants More Death

death wants more death, and its webs are full:
I remember my father's garage, how child-like
I would brush the corpses of flies
from the windows they had thought were escape—
their sticky, ugly, vibrant bodies
shouting like dumb crazy dogs against the glass
only to spin and flit
in that second larger than hell or heaven
onto the edge of the ledge,
and then the spider from his dank hole
nervous and exposed
the puff of body swelling
hanging there
not really quite knowing,
and then *knowing*—
something sending it down its string,
the wet web,
toward the weak shield of buzzing,
the pulsing;
a last desperate moving hair-leg
there against the glass
there alive in the sun,
spun in white;

and almost like love:
the closing over,
the first hushed spider-sucking:
filling its sack
upon this thing that lived;
crouching there upon its back
drawing its certain blood
as the world goes by outside

and my temples scream
and I hurl the broom against them:
the spider dull with spider-anger
still thinking of its prey
and waving an amazed broken leg;
the fly very still,
a dirty speck stranded to straw;
I shake the killer loose
and he walks lame and peeved
towards some dark corner
but I intercept his dawdling
his crawling like some broken hero,
and the straws smash his legs
now waving
above his head
and looking
looking for the enemy
and somehow valiant,
dying without apparent pain
simply crawling backward
piece by piece
leaving nothing there
until at last the red gut-sack splashes
its secrets,
and I run child-like
with God's anger a step behind,
back to simple sunlight,
wondering
as the world goes by
with curled smile
if anyone else
saw or sensed my crime.

the lisp

I had her for 3 units
and at mid-term
she'd read off how many assignments
stories
had been turned in:
"Gilbert: 2 . . .
Ginsing: 5 . . .
McNulty: 4 . . .
Frijoles: none . . .
Lansford: 2 . . .
Bukowski: 38 . . ."

the class laughed
and she lisped
that not only did Bukowski
write many stories
but that they were all of
high quality.

she flashed her golden legs
in 1940 and there was something
sexy about her lisp
sexy as a hornet
as a rattler
that lisp.

and she lisped to me
after class
that I should go to
war,
that I would make a
very good sailor,

and she told me about how
she took my stories home
and read them to her husband
and how they both laughed,
and I told her, "o.k., Mrs. Anderson."
and I'd walk out on the campus
where almost every guy had a
girl.

I didn't become a sailor,
Mrs. Anderson, I'm not crazy
about the ocean
and I didn't like war
even when it was the popular
thing to
do.

but here's another completed assignment
for you
those golden legs
that lisp
still has me typing
love songs.

on being 20

my mother knocked on my rooming-house door
and came in
looked in the dresser drawer:
"Henry you don't have any clean
stockings?
do you change your underwear?"

"Mom, I don't want you poking around in
here . . ."

"I hear that there is a woman
who comes to your room late at
night and she drinks with you, she lives
right down the hall."

"she's all right . . ."

"Henry, you can get a terrible
disease."

"yeah . . ."

"I talked with your landlady, she's a
nice lady, she says you must read a lot
of books in bed because as you fall to sleep at
night the books fall to the floor,
they can hear it all over the
house, heavy books, one at midnight,
another at one a.m., another at 2 a.m.,
another at four."

after she left I took the library books
back
returned to the rooming house and
put the dirty stockings and the dirty
underwear and the dirty shirts into
the paper suitcase
took the streetcar downtown
boarded the Trailways bus to
New Orleans
figuring to arrive with ten dollars
and let them do with me
what they would.

they did.

meanwhile

neither does this mean
the dead are
at the door
begging bread
before
the stockpiles
blow
like all the
storms and hell
in one big love,
but anyhow
I rented a 6 dollar a week
room
in Chinatown
with a window as large as the
side of the world
filled with night flies and neon,
lighted like Broadway
to frighten away rats,
and I walked into a bar and sat down,
and the Chinaman looked at my rags
and said
no credit
and I pulled out a hundred-dollar bill
and asked for a cup of Confucius juice
and 2 China dolls with slits of eyes
just about the size of the rest of them
slid closer
and we sat
and we
waited.

the world's greatest loser

he used to sell papers in front:
"Get your winners! Get rich on a dime!"
and about the 3rd or 4th race
you'd see him rolling in on his rotten board
with roller skates underneath.
he'd propel himself along on his hands;
he just had small stumps for legs
and the rims of the skate wheels were worn off.
you could see inside the wheels and they would wobble
something awful
shooting and flashing
imperialistic sparks!
he moved faster than anybody, rolled cigarette dangling,
you could hear him coming
"god o mighty, what was that?" the new ones asked.

he was the world's greatest loser
but he never gave up
wheeling toward the 2-dollar window screaming:
"IT'S THE 4 HORSE, YOU FOOLS! HOW THE HELL YA
GONNA BEAT THE
4?"
up on the board the 4 would be reading
60 to 1.
I never heard him pick a winner.

they say he slept in the bushes. I guess that's where he
died. he's not around any
more.

there was the big fat blonde whore
who kept touching him for luck, and
laughing.

nobody had any luck. the whore is gone
too.

I guess nothing ever works for us. we're fools, of course—
bucking the inside plus a 15 percent take,
but how are you going to tell a dreamer
there's a 15 percent take on the
dream? he'll just laugh and say,
is that all?

I miss those
sparks.

human nature

it has been going on for some time.
there is this young waitress where I get my coffee
at the racetrack.
"how are you doing today?" she asks.
"winning pretty good," I reply.
"you won yesterday, didn't you?" she
asks.
"yes," I say, "and the day before."

I don't know exactly what it is but I
believe we must have incompatible
personalities. there is often a hostile
undertone to our conversations.

"you seem to be the only person
around here who keeps winning,"
she says, not looking at me,
not pleased.

"is that so?" I answer.

there is something very strange about all
this: whenever I do lose
she never seems to be
there.
perhaps it's her day off or sometimes she works
another counter?

she bets too and loses.
she always loses.
and even though we might have
incompatible personalities I am sorry for

her.
I decide the next time I see her
I will tell her that I am
losing.

so I do.
when she asks, "how are you doing?"
I say, "god, I don't understand it,
I'm losing, I can't hit anything, every horse
I bet runs last!"

"really?" she asks.
"really," I say.

it works.
she lowers her gaze
and here comes one of the largest smiles
I have ever seen, it damn near cracks
her face wide open.

I get my coffee, tip her well, walk
out to check the
toteboard.

if I died in a flaming crash on the freeway
she'd surely be happy for a
week!

I take a sip of coffee.
what's this?
she's put in a large shot of cream!
she knows I like it black!

in her excitement,
she'd forgotten.

the bitch.

and that's what I get for lying.

the trash men

here they come
these guys
gray truck
radio playing

they are in a hurry

it's quite exciting:
shirt open
bellies hanging out

they run out the trash bins
roll them out to the fork lift
and then the truck grinds it upward
with far too much sound . . .

they had to fill out application forms
to get these jobs
they are paying for homes and
drive late model cars

they get drunk on Saturday night

now in the Los Angeles sunshine
they run back and forth with their trash bins

all that trash goes somewhere

and they shout to each other

then they are all up in the truck
driving west toward the sea

none of them know
that I am alive

REX DISPOSAL CO.

a gold pocket watch

my grandfather was a tall German
with a strange smell on his breath.
he stood very straight
in front of his small house
and his wife hated him
and his children thought him odd.
I was six the first time we met
and he gave me all his war medals.
the second time I met him
he gave me his gold pocket watch.
it was very heavy and I took it home
and wound it very tight
and it stopped running
which made me feel bad.
I never saw him again
and my parents never spoke of him
nor did my grandmother
who had long ago
stopped living with him.
once I asked about him
and they told me
he drank too much
but I liked him best
standing very straight
in front of his house
and saying, "hello, Henry, you
and I, we know each
other."

talking to my mailbox . . .

boy, don't come around here telling me you
can't cut it, that
they're pitching you low and inside, that
they are conspiring against you,
that all you want is a chance but they won't
give you a
chance.

boy, the problem is that you're not doing
what you want to do, or
if you're doing what you want to do, you're
just not doing it
well.

boy, I agree:
there's not much opportunity, and there are
some at the top who are
not doing much better than you
are
but
you're wasting energy haranguing and
bitching.

boy, I'm not *advising*, just suggesting that
instead of sending your poems to me
along with your letters of
complaint
you should enter the
arena—
send your work to the editors and
publishers, it will

buck up your backbone and your
versatility.

boy, I wish to thank you for the
praise for some of my
published works
but that
has nothing to do with
anything and won't help a
purple shit, you've just got to
learn to hit that low, hard
inside pitch.

this is a form letter
I send to almost everybody, but
I hope you take it
personally,
man.

I liked him

I liked D. H. Lawrence
he could get so indignant
he snapped and he ripped
with wonderfully energetic sentences
he could lay the word down
bright and writhing
there was the stink of blood and murder
and sacrifice about him
the only tenderness he allowed
was when he bedded down his large German
wife.
I liked D. H. Lawrence—
he could talk about Christ
like he was the man next door
and he could describe Australian taxi drivers
so well you hated them
I liked D. H. Lawrence
but I'm glad I never met him
in some bistro
him lifting his tiny hot cup of
tea
and looking at me
with his worm-hole eyes.

one for the shoeshine man

the balance is preserved by the snails climbing the
Santa Monica cliffs;
the luck is in walking down Western Avenue
and having the girls in a massage
parlor holler at you, "Hello, Sweetie!"
the miracle is having 5 women in love
with you at the age of 55,
and the goodness is that you are only able
to love one of them.
the gift is having a daughter more gentle
than you are, whose laughter is finer
than yours.
the peace comes from driving a
blue 67 Volks through the streets like a
teenager, radio tuned to The Host Who Loves You
Most, feeling the sun, feeling the solid hum
of the rebuilt motor
as you needle through traffic.
the grace is being able to like rock music,
symphony music, jazz . . .
anything that contains the original energy of
joy.

and the probability that returns
is the deep blue low
yourself flat upon yourself
within the guillotine walls
angry at the sound of the phone
or anybody's footsteps passing;
but the other probability—
the lilting high that always follows—
makes the girl at the checkstand in the

supermarket look like
Marilyn
like Jackie before they got her Harvard lover
like the girl in high school that we
all followed home.

there is that which helps you believe
in something else besides death:
somebody in a car approaching
on a street too narrow,
and he or she pulls aside to let you
by, or the old fighter Beau Jack
shining shoes
after blowing the entire bankroll
on parties
on women
on parasites,
humming, breathing on the leather,
working the rag
looking up and saying:
"what the hell, I had it for a
while. that beats the
other."

I am bitter sometimes
but the taste has often been
sweet. it's only that I've
feared to say it. it's like
when your woman says,
"tell me you love me," and
you can't.

if you see me grinning from
my blue Volks
running a yellow light
driving straight into the sun
I will be locked in the
arms of a
crazy life
thinking of trapeze artists
of midgets with big cigars
of a Russian winter in the early 40s
of Chopin with his bag of Polish soil
of an old waitress bringing me an extra
cup of coffee and laughing
as she does so.

the best of you
I like more than you think.
the others don't count
except that they have fingers and heads
and some of them eyes
and most of them legs
and all of them
good and bad dreams
and a way to go.

justice is everywhere and it's working
and the machine guns and the frogs
and the hedges will tell you
so.

the proud
thin
dying

I see old people on pensions in the
supermarkets and they are thin and they are
proud and they are dying
they are starving on their feet and saying
nothing. long ago, among other lies,
they were taught that silence was
bravery. now, having worked a lifetime,
inflation has trapped them. they look around
steal a grape
chew on it. finally they make a tiny
purchase, a day's worth.
another lie they were taught:
thou shalt not steal.
they'd rather starve than steal
(one grape won't save them)
and in tiny rooms
while reading the market ads
they'll starve
they'll die without a sound
pulled out of rooming houses
by young blond boys with long hair
who'll slide them in
and pull away from the curb, these
boys
handsome of eye
thinking of Vegas and pussy and
victory.
it's the order of things: each one
gets a taste of honey
then the knife.

shot of red-eye

I used to hold my social security card
up in the air,
he told me,
but I was so small
they couldn't see it,
all those big
guys around.

you mean the place with the
big green screen?
I asked.

yeah. well, anyhow, I finally got on
the other day
picking tomatoes, and Jesus Christ,
I couldn't get anywhere
it was too hot, too hot
and I couldn't get anything in my sack
so I lay under the truck
in the shade and drank
wine. I didn't make a
dime.

have a drink, I said.

sure, he said.

two big women came in and
I mean BIG
and they sat next to
us.

shot of red-eye, one of them
said to the bartender.

likewise, said the other.

they pulled their dresses up
around their hips and
swung their legs.

um, umm. I think I'm going mad, I told
my friend from the tomato fields.

Jesus, he said, Jesus and Mary, I can't
believe what I see.

it's all
there, I said.

you a fighter? the one next to me
asked.

no, I said.

what happened to your
face?

automobile accident on the San Berdoo
freeway. some drunk jumped the divider. I was
the drunk.

how old *are* you, daddy?

old enough to slice the melon, I said,
tapping my cigar ashes into my beer to give me
strength.

can you buy a melon? she asked.

have you ever been chased across the Mojave and
raped?

no, she said.

I pulled out my last 20 and with an old man's
virile abandon ordered
four drinks.

both girls smiled and pulled their dresses
higher, if that was possible.

who's your friend? they asked.

this is Lord Chesterfield, I told them.

pleased ta meetcha, they
said.

hello, bitches, he answered.

we walked through the 3rd street tunnel
to a green hotel. the girls had a
key.

there was one bed and we all got
in. I don't know who got
who.

the next morning my friend and I
were down at the Farm Labor Market
on San Pedro Street
holding up and waving our social
security cards.

they couldn't see
his.

I was the last one on the truck out. a big woman stood
up against me. she smelled like
port wine.

honey, she asked, whatever happened to your
face?

fair grounds, a dancing bear who
didn't.

bullshit, she said.

maybe so, I said, but get your hand out
from around my
balls. everybody's looking.

when we got to the
fields the sun was
really up
and the world
looked
terrible.

about pain

my first and only wife
painted
and she talked to me
about it:
"it's all so *painful*
for me, each stroke is
pain . . .
one mistake and
the whole painting is
ruined . . .
you will *never* under-
stand the
pain . . ."

"look, baby," I
said, "why doncha do something easy—
something ya like ta
do?"

she just looked at me
and I think it was her
first understanding of
the tragedy of our being
together.

such things usually
begin
somewhere.

hot

she was hot, she was so hot
I didn't want anybody else to have her,
and if I didn't get home on time
she'd be gone, and I couldn't bear that—
I'd go mad . . .
it was foolish I know, childish,
but I was caught in it, I was caught.

I delivered all the mail
and then Henderson put me on the night pickup run
in an old army truck,
the damn thing began to heat halfway through the run
and the night went on
me thinking about my hot Miriam
and jumping in and out of the truck
filling mailsacks
the engine continuing to heat up
the temperature needle was at the top
HOT   HOT
like Miriam.

I leaped in and out
3 more pickups and into the station
I'd be, my car
waiting to get me to Miriam who sat on my blue couch
with scotch on the rocks
crossing her legs and swinging her ankles
like she did,
2 more stops . . .
the truck stalled at a traffic light, it was hell
kicking it over

again . . .
I had to be home by 8, 8 was the deadline for Miriam.

I made the last pickup and the truck stalled at a signal
½ block from the station . . .
it wouldn't start, it couldn't start . . .
I locked the doors, pulled the key and ran down to the
station . . .
I threw the keys down. . . . signed out . . .
your goddamned truck is stalled at the signal,
I shouted,
Pico and Western . . .

. . . I ran down the hall, put the key into the door,
opened it. . . . her drinking glass was there, and a note:

> *sun of a bitch:*
> *I wated until 5 after ate*
> *you don't love me*
> *you sun of a bitch*
> *somebody will love me*
> *I been wateing all day*

> *Miriam*

I poured a drink and let the water run into the tub
there were 5,000 bars in town
and I'd make 25 of them
looking for Miriam

her purple teddy bear held the note
as he leaned against a pillow

I gave the bear a drink, myself a drink
and got into the hot
water.

who in the hell is
Tom Jones?

I was shacked with a
24-year-old girl from
New York City for
two weeks—about
the time of the garbage
strike out there, and
one night my 34-year-
old woman arrived and
she said, "I want to see
my rival." she did
and then she said, "o,
you're a cute little thing!"
next I knew there was a
screech of wildcats—
such screaming and scratch-
ing, wounded animal moans,
blood and piss . . .

I was drunk and in my
shorts. I tried to
separate them and fell,
wrenched my knee. then
they were through the screen
door and down the walk
and out in the street.

squad cars full of cops
arrived. a police heli-
copter circled overhead.

I stood in the bathroom
and grinned in the mirror.
it's not often at the age
of 55 that such splendid
things occur.
better than the Watts
riots.

the 34-year-old
came back in. she had
pissed all over her-
self and her clothing
was torn and she was
followed by 2 cops who
wanted to know why.

pulling up my shorts
I tried to explain.

the price

drinking 15-dollar champagne—
Cordon Rouge—with the hookers.

one is named Georgia and she
doesn't like pantyhose:
I keep helping her pull up
her long dark stockings.

the other is Pam—prettier
but not much soul, and
we smoke and talk and I
play with their legs and
stick my bare foot into
Georgia's open purse.
it's filled with
bottles of pills. I
take some of the pills.

"listen," I say, "one of
you has soul, the other
looks. can't I combine
the 2 of you? take the soul
and stick it into the looks?"

"you want me," says Pam, "it
will cost you a hundred."

we drink some more and Georgia
falls to the floor and can't
get up.

I tell Pam that I like her
earrings very much. her
hair is long and a natural
red.

"I was only kidding about the
hundred," she says.

"oh," I say, "what will it cost
me?"

she lights her cigarette with
my lighter and looks at me
through the flame:

her eyes tell me.

"look," I say, "I don't think I
can ever pay that price again."

she crosses her legs
inhales on her cigarette

as she exhales she smiles
and says, "sure you can."

I'm in love

she's young, she said,
but look at me,
I have pretty ankles,
and look at my wrists, I have pretty
wrists
o my god,
I thought it was all working,
and now it's her again,
every time she phones you go crazy,
you told me it was over
you told me it was finished,
listen, I've lived long enough to become a
good woman,
why do you need a bad woman?
you need to be tortured, don't you?
you think life is rotten if somebody treats you
rotten it all fits,
doesn't it?
tell me, is that it? do you want to be treated like a
piece of shit?
and my son, my son was going to meet you.
I told my son
and I dropped all my lovers.
I stood up in a cafe and screamed
I'M IN LOVE,
and now you've made a fool of me . . .

I'm sorry, I said, I'm really sorry.

hold me, she said, will you please hold me?

499

I've never been in one of these things before, I said,
these triangles . . .

she got up and lit a cigarette, she was trembling all
over. she paced up and down, wild and crazy. she had
a small body. her arms were thin, very thin and when
she screamed and started beating me I held her
wrists and then I got it through the eyes: hatred,
centuries deep and true. I was wrong and graceless and
sick. all the things I had learned had been wasted.
there was no living creature as foul as I
and all my poems were
false.

the girls

I have been looking at
the same
lampshade
for
    5 years
and it has gathered
a bachelor's dust
and
the girls who enter here
are too
busy
to clean it

but I don't mind
I have been too
busy
to notice
until now

that the light
shines
badly
        through
    5 years'
worth.

the ladies of summer

the ladies of summer will die like the rose
and the lie

the ladies of summer will love
so long as the price is not
forever

the ladies of summer
might love anybody;
they might even love you
as long as summer
lasts

yet winter will come to them
too

white snow and
a cold freezing
and faces so ugly
that even death
will turn away—
wince—
before taking
them.

tonight

"your poems about the girls will still be around
50 years from now when the girls are gone,"
my editor phones me.

dear editor:
the girls appear to be gone
already.

I know what you mean

but give me one truly alive woman
tonight
walking across the floor toward me

and you can have all the poems

the good ones
the bad ones
or any that I might write
after this one.

I know what you mean.

do you know what I mean?

shoes

when you're young
a pair of
female
high-heeled shoes
just sitting
alone
in the closet
can fire your
bones;
when you're old
it's just
a pair of shoes
without
anybody
in them
and
just as
well.

hug the dark

turmoil is the god
madness is the god

permanent living peace is
permanent living death.

agony can kill
or
agony can sustain life
but peace is always horrifying
peace is the worst thing
walking
talking
smiling,
seeming to be.

don't forget the sidewalks
the whores,
betrayal,
the worm in the apple,
the bars, the jails,
the suicides of lovers.

here in America
we have assassinated a president and his brother,
another president has quit office.

people who believe in politics
are like people who believe in god:
they are sucking wind through bent
straws.

there is no god
there are no politics
there is no peace
there is no love
there is no control
there is no plan

stay away from god
remain disturbed

slide.

face of a political candidate on a street billboard

there he is:
not too many hangovers
not too many fights with women
not too many flat tires
never a thought of suicide

not more than three toothaches
never missed a meal
never in jail
never in love

7 pairs of shoes

a son in college

a car one year old

insurance policies

a very green lawn

garbage cans with tight lids

he'll be elected.

white dog

I went for a walk on Hollywood Boulevard.
I looked down and there was a large white dog
walking beside me.
his pace was exactly the same as mine.
we stopped at traffic signals together.
we crossed the side streets together.
a woman smiled at us.
he must have walked 8 blocks with me.
then I went into a grocery store and
when I came out he was gone.
or she was gone.
the wonderful white dog
with a trace of yellow in its fur.
the large blue eyes were gone.
the grinning mouth was gone.
the lolling tongue was gone.

things are so easily lost.
things just can't be kept forever.

I got the blues.
I got the blues.
that dog loved and
trusted me and
I let it walk away.

on going out to get the mail

the droll noon
where squadrons of worms creep up like
stripteasers
to be raped by blackbirds.

I go outside
and all up and down the street
the green armies shoot color
like an everlasting 4th of July,
and I too seem to swell inside,
a kind of unknown bursting, a
feeling, perhaps, that there isn't any
enemy
anywhere.

and I reach down into the box
and there is
nothing—not even a
letter from the gas co. saying they will
shut it off
again.

not even a short note from my x-wife
bragging about her present
happiness.

my hand searches the mailbox in a kind of
disbelief long after the mind has
given up.

there's not even a dead fly
down in there.

I am a fool, I think, I should have known it
works like this.

I go inside as all the flowers leap to
please me.

anything? the woman
asks.

nothing, I answer, what's for
breakfast?

spring swan

swans die in the Spring too
and there it floated
dead on a Sunday
sideways
circling in the current
and I walked to the rotunda
and overhead
gods in chariots
dogs, women
circled,
and death
ran down my throat
like a mouse,
and I heard the people coming
with their picnic bags
and laughter,
and I felt guilty
for the swan
as if death
were a thing of shame
and like a fool
I walked away
and left them
my beautiful swan.

how is your heart?

during my worst times
on the park benches
in the jails
or living with
whores
I always had this certain
contentment—
I wouldn't call it
happiness—
it was more of an inner
balance
that settled for
whatever was occurring
and it helped in the
factories
and when relationships
went wrong
with the
girls.

it helped
through the
wars and the
hangovers
the backalley fights
the
hospitals.

to awaken in a cheap room
in a strange city and
pull up the shade—

this was the craziest kind of
contentment

and to walk across the floor
to an old dresser with a
cracked mirror—
see myself, ugly,
grinning at it all.

what matters most is
how well you
walk through the
fire.

closing time

around 2 a.m.
in my small room
after turning off the poem
machine
for now
I continue to light
cigarettes and listen to
Beethoven on the
radio.
I listen with a
strange and lazy
aplomb,
knowing there's still a poem
or two left to write, and
I feel damn
fine, at long
last,
as once again I
admire the verve and gamble
of this composer
now dead for over 100
years,
who's younger and wilder
than you are
than I am.

the centuries are sprinkled
with rare magic
with divine creatures
who help us get past the common
and

extraordinary ills
that beset us.

I light the next to last
cigarette
remember all the 2 a.m.s
of my past,
put out of the bars
at closing time,
put out on the streets
(a ragged band of
solitary lonely
humans
we were)
each walking home
alone.

this is much better: living
where I now
live
and listening to
the reassurance
the kindness
of this unexpected
SYMPHONY OF TRIUMPH:
a new life.

racetrack parking lot
at the end of the day

I watch them push the crippled and the infirm
in their wheelchairs
on to the electric lift
which carries them up into the long bus
where each chair is locked down
and each person has a window
of their own.
they are all white-skinned, like
pale paint on thin cardboard;
most of them are truly old;
there are a number of women, a few old
men, and 3 surprisingly young men
2 of whom wear neck braces that *gleam*
in the late afternoon sun
and all 3 with arms as thin as
rope and hands that resemble clenched
claws.
the caretaker seems very kind, very
understanding, he's a
marvelous fat fellow with a
rectangular head and he wears a broad
smile which is not
false.
the old women are either extremely thin
or overweight.
most have humped backs and shoulders
and wispy
very straight
white hair.
they sit motionless, look straight
ahead as the electric lift raises them

on to the bus.
there is no conversation;
they appear calm and not embittered
by their plight. both men and women
are soon loaded on to the waiting bus except for
the last one, a very old man, almost skeletal,
with a tiny round head, completely bald, a
shining white dot against the late afternoon sky,
waving a cane above his head as he is
pushed shouting on to the electric lift:
"WELL, THEY ROBBED OUR ASSES
AGAIN, CLEANED US OUT, WE'RE A
BUNCH OF SUCKERS TOTTERING ON THE
EDGE OF OUR GRAVES AND WE LET THEM TAKE
OUR LAST PENNY AGAIN!"
as he speaks
he waves the cane above his head and
cracks the marvelous fat fellow
who is pushing his chair,
cracks the cane against the side of
the caretaker's head.
it's a mighty blow and
the attendant staggers, grabs
hard at the back of the
wheelchair
as the old man yells: "OH, JERRY,
I'M SORRY, I'M SO SORRY, WHAT CAN I
DO? WHAT
CAN I DO?"

Jerry steadies himself, he is not badly hurt.
it's a small concussion but within an hour
he will possess a knot the size of an
apricot.

"it's all right, Sandy, only
I've told you again and again, please
be careful with that damned
cane . . ."

Sandy is pushed on to the electric
lift, it rises and he disappears into
the bus's dark interior.

then Jerry climbs slowly into the bus, takes
the wheel, starts up, the door closes with a hiss,
the bus begins to move to the exit,
and on the back of the vehicle
in bold white letters
on dark blue background
I see the words:
HARBOR HOME OF LOVE.

there

the centerfielder
turns
rushes back
reaches up his glove
and
snares the
ball,
we are all him for
that moment,
sucking the air
into our
gut.
as the crowd roars like
crazy
we rifle the ball back
through the
miraculous
air.

Dinosauria, we

born like this
into this
as the chalk faces smile
as Mrs. Death laughs
as the elevators break
as political landscapes dissolve
as the supermarket bag boy holds a college degree
as the oily fish spit out their oily prey
as the sun is masked

we are
born like this
into this
into these carefully mad wars
into the sight of broken factory windows of emptiness
into bars where people no longer speak to each other
into fist fights that end as shootings and knifings

born into this
into hospitals which are so expensive that it's cheaper to die
into lawyers who charge so much it's cheaper to plead guilty
into a country where the jails are full and the madhouses closed
into a place where the masses elevate fools into rich heroes

born into this
walking and living through this
dying because of this
muted because of this
castrated
debauched
disinherited

because of this
fooled by this
used by this
pissed on by this
made crazy and sick by this
made violent
made inhuman
by this

the heart is blackened
the fingers reach for the throat
the gun
the knife
the bomb
the fingers reach toward an unresponsive god

the fingers reach for the bottle
the pill
the powder

we are born into this sorrowful deadliness
we are born into a government 60 years in debt
that soon will be unable to even pay the interest on that debt
and the banks will burn
money will be useless
there will be open and unpunished murder in the streets
it will be guns and roving mobs
land will be useless
food will become a diminishing return
nuclear power will be taken over by the many
explosions will continually shake the earth

radiated robot men will stalk each other
the rich and the chosen will watch from space platforms
Dante's Inferno will be made to look like a children's playground

the sun will not be seen and it will always be night
trees will die
all vegetation will die
radiated men will eat the flesh of radiated men
the sea will be poisoned
the lakes and rivers will vanish
rain will be the new gold

the rotting bodies of men and animals will stink in the dark wind

the last few survivors will be overtaken by new and hideous diseases
and the space platforms will be destroyed by attrition
the petering out of supplies
the natural effect of general decay

and there will be the most beautiful silence never heard

born out of that.

the sun still hidden there

awaiting the next chapter.

mind and heart

unaccountably we are alone
forever alone
and it was meant to be
that way,
it was never meant
to be any other way—
and when the death struggle
begins
the last thing I wish to see
is
a ring of human faces
hovering over me—
better just my old friends,
the walls of my self,
let only them be there.

I have been alone but seldom
lonely.
I have satisfied my thirst
at the well
of my self
and that wine was good,
the best I ever had,
and tonight
sitting
staring into the dark
I now finally understand
the dark and the
light and everything
in between.

peace of mind and heart
arrives
when we accept what
is:
having been
born into this
strange life
we must accept
the wasted gamble of our
days
and take some satisfaction in
the pleasure of
leaving it all
behind.

cry not for me.

grieve not for me.

read
what I've written
then
forget it
all.

drink from the well
of your self
and begin
again.

TB

I had it for a year, really put in
a lot of
bedroom time, slept upright on
two pillows to keep from coughing,
all the blood drained from my head
and often I'd awaken to find myself
slipping sideways off the
bed.
since my TB was contagious I didn't
have any visitors and the phone
stopped ringing
and that was the lucky
part.

during the day I tried TV and food,
neither of which went down very
well.
the soap operas and the talk shows
were a
daytime nightmare,
so for the lack of anything else
to do
I watched the baseball
games
and led the Dodgers to a
pennant.
not much else for me to do
except take antibiotics and the cough
medicine.
I also really saved putting
mileage on the car
and missed the hell out of

the old race
track.

you realize when you're
plucked out of the mainstream that
it doesn't need you or
anybody else.
the birds don't notice you're gone,
the flowers don't care,
the people out there don't notice,
but the IRS,
the phone co.,
the gas and electric co.,
the DMV, etc.,
they keep in touch.

being very sick and being dead are
very much the same
in society's
eye.

either way,
you might just as well
lay back and
enjoy it.

crime does pay

the rooms at the hospital went for
$550 a day.
that was for the room alone.
the amazing thing, though, was that
in some of the rooms
prisoners were
lodged.
I saw them chained to their beds,
usually by an
ankle.
$550 a day, plus meals,
now that's luxury
living—plus first-rate medical attention
and two guards
on watch.
and here I was with my cancer,
walking down the halls in my
robe
thinking, if I live through this
it will take me years to
pay off the hospital
while the prisoners won't owe
a damned
thing.
not that I didn't have some
sympathy for those fellows
but when you consider that
when something like a bullet
in one of your buttocks
gets you all that free attention,
medical and otherwise,

plus no billing later
from the hospital business
office, maybe I had chosen
the wrong
occupation?

the orderly

I am sitting on a tin chair outside the x-ray lab as
death, on stinking wings, wafts through the
halls forevermore.
I remember the hospital stenches from when
I was a boy and when I was a man and now
as an old man
I sit in my tin chair waiting.

then an orderly
a young man of 23 or 24
pushes in a piece of equipment.
it looks like a hamper of
freshly done laundry
but I can't be sure.

the orderly is awkward.
he is not deformed
but his legs work
in an unruly fashion
as if disassociated from the
motor workings of the brain.

he is in blue, dressed all in blue,
pushing,
pushing his load.

ungainly little boy blue.

then he turns his head and yells at
the receptionist at the x-ray window:
"anybody wants me, I'll be in 76
for about 20 minutes!"

his face reddens as he yells,
his mouth forms a down
turned crescent like a
pumpkin's halloween mouth.

then he's gone into some doorway,
probably 76.

not a very *prepossessing* chap.
lost as a human,
long gone down some
numbing road.

but
he's healthy

he's healthy.

HE'S HEALTHY!

the nurses

at the hospital that I have been
going to
the nurses seem
overweight.
they are bulky in their
white dresses
fat above the hips
and down
through the buttocks
to the heavy
legs.

they all appear to be
47 years old,
walk wide-legged
like the old fullbacks
of the
1930s.

they seem distanced
from their profession.
they attend to their duties
but with a
lack of
contact.

I pass them in the
walkways
and in the
corridors.
they never look into
my eyes.

I forgive them their
heavy-shoed
walk,
for the space that they
must forge
between themselves and
each patient.

for these ladies are truly
over-fed:

they have seen
too much
death.

cancer

half-past nowhere
alone
in the crumbling
tower of myself

stumbling in this the
darkest
hour

the last gamble has been
lost

as I
reach
for

bone
silence.

first poem back

64 days and nights in that
place, chemotherapy,
antibiotics, blood running into
the catheter.
leukemia.
who, me?
at age 72 I had this foolish thought that
I'd just die peacefully in my sleep
but
the gods want it their way.
I sit at this machine, shattered,
half alive,
still seeking the Muse,
but I am back for the moment only;
while nothing seems the same.
I am not reborn, only
chasing
a few more days, a few more nights,
like
this
one.

tired in the afterdusk

smoking a cigarette and noting a mosquito who has
flattened out against the wall and
died
as organ music from centuries back plays through
my black radio
as downstairs my wife watches a rented video on
the VCR.

this is the space between spaces, this is when the
ever-war relents for just a moment, this is when
you consider the inconsiderate years:
the fight has been wearing . . . but, at times,
interesting, such as
resting quietly here in the
afterdusk as the sound of the centuries run
through my body . . .
this
old dog
resting in the shade
peaceful
but ready.

again

now the territory is taken,
the sacrificial lambs have been slain,
as history is scratched again on the sallow walls,
as the bankers scurry to survive,
as the young girls paint their hungry lips,
as the dogs sleep in temporary peace,
as the shadow gets ready to fall,
as the oceans gobble the poisons of man,
as heaven and hell dance in the anteroom,
it's begin again and go again,
it's bake the apple,
buy the car,
mow the lawn,
pay the tax,
hang the toilet paper,
clip the nails,
listen to the crickets,
blow up the balloons,
drink the orange juice,
forget the past,
pass the mustard,
pull down the shades,
take the pills,
check the air in the tires,
lace on the gloves,
the bell is ringing,
the pearl is in the oyster,
the rain falls
as the shadow gets ready to fall again.

so now?

the words have come and gone,
I sit ill.
the phone rings, the cats sleep.
Linda vacuums.
I am waiting to live,
waiting to die.

I wish I could ring in some bravery.
it's a lousy fix
but the tree outside doesn't know:
I watch it moving with the wind
in the late afternoon sun.

there's nothing to declare here,
just a waiting.
each faces it alone.

Oh, I was once young,
Oh, I was once unbelievably
young!

blue

blue fish, the blue night, a blue knife—
everything is blue.
and my cats are blue: blue fur, blue claws,
blue whiskers, blue eyes.

my bed lamp shines
blue.

inside, my blue heart pumps blue blood.

my fingernails, my toenails are
blue

and around my bed floats a
blue ghost.

even the taste inside my mouth is
blue.

and I am alone and dying and
blue.

a summation

more wasted days,
gored days,
evaporated days.

more squandered days,
days pissed away,
days slapped around,
mutilated.

the problem is
that the days add up
to a life,
my life.

I sit here
73 years old
knowing I have been badly
fooled,
picking at my teeth
with a toothpick
which
breaks.

dying should come easy:
like a freight train you
don't hear when
your back is
turned.

sun coming down

no one is sorry I am leaving,
not even I;
but there should be a minstrel
or at least a glass of wine.

it bothers the young most, I think:
an unviolent slow death.
still it makes any man dream;
you wish for an old sailing ship,
the white salt-crusted sail
and the sea shaking out hints of immortality.

sea in the nose
sea in the hair
sea in the marrow, in the eyes
and yes, there in the chest.
will we miss
the love of a woman or music or food
or the gambol of the great mad muscled
horse, kicking clods and destinies
high and away
in just one moment of the sun coming down?

but now it's my turn
and there's no majesty in it
because there was no majesty
before it
and each of us, like worms bitten
    out of apples,
deserves no reprieve.

death enters my mouth
and snakes along my teeth
and I wonder if I am frightened of
this voiceless, unsorrowful dying that is
like the drying of a rose?

twilight musings

the drifting of the mind.

the slow loss, the leaking away.

one's demise is not very interesting.

from my bed I watch 3 birds through the east window:

one coal black, one dark brown, the

other yellow.

as night falls I watch the red lights on the bridge blink on and off.

I am stretched out in bed with the covers up to my chin.

I have no idea who won at the racetrack today.

I must go back into the hospital tomorrow.

why me?

why not?

my last winter

I see this final storm as nothing very serious in the sight of
the world;
there are so many more important things to worry about and to
consider.

I see this final storm as nothing very special in the sight of
the world
and it shouldn't be thought of as special.
other storms have been much greater, more dramatic.
I see this final storm approaching and calmly
my mind waits.

I see this final storm as nothing very serious in the sight of
the world.
the world and I have seldom agreed on most
matters but
now we can agree.
so bring it on, bring on this final storm.
I have patiently waited for too long now.

like a dolphin

dying has its rough edge.
no escaping now.
the warden has his eye on me.
his bad eye.
I'm doing hard time now.
in solitary.
locked down.
I'm not the first nor the last.
I'm just telling you how it is.
I sit in my own shadow now.
the face of the people grows dim.
the old songs still play.
hand to my chin, I dream of
nothing while my lost childhood
leaps like a dolphin
in the frozen sea.

the bluebird

there's a bluebird in my heart that
wants to get out
but I'm too tough for him,
I say, stay in there, I'm not going
to let anybody see
you.

there's a bluebird in my heart that
wants to get out
but I pour whiskey on him and inhale
cigarette smoke
and the whores and the bartenders
and the grocery clerks
never know that
he's
in there.

there's a bluebird in my heart that
wants to get out
but I'm too tough for him,
I say,
stay down, do you want to mess
me up?
you want to screw up the
works?
you want to blow my book sales in
Europe?

there's a bluebird in my heart that
wants to get out
but I'm too clever, I only let him out
at night sometimes

when everybody's asleep.
I say, I know that you're there,
so don't be
sad.

then I put him back,
but he's singing a little
in there, I haven't quite let him
die
and we sleep together like
that
with our
secret pact
and it's nice enough to
make a man
weep, but I don't
weep, do
you?

if we take—

if we take what we can see—
the engines driving us mad,
lovers finally hating;
this fish in the market
staring upward into our minds;
flowers rotting, flies web-caught;
riots, roars of caged lions,
clowns in love with dollar bills,
nations moving people like pawns;
daylight thieves with beautiful
nighttime wives and wines;
the crowded jails,
the commonplace unemployed,
dying grass, 2-bit fires;
men old enough to love the grave.

These things, and others, in content
show life swinging on a rotten axis.

But they've left us a bit of music
and a spiked show in the corner,
a jigger of scotch, a blue necktie,
a small volume of poems by Rimbaud,
a horse running as if the devil were
twisting his tail
over bluegrass and screaming, and then,
love again
like a streetcar turning the corner
on time,

the city waiting,
the wine and the flowers,
the water walking across the lake
and summer and winter and summer and summer
and winter again.

alphabetical index of poem titles

CHARLES BUKOWSKI is one of America's best-known contemporary writers of poetry and prose, and, many would claim, its most influential and imitated poet. He was born in Andernach, Germany, to an American soldier father and a German mother in 1920, and brought to the United States at the age of three. He was raised in Los Angeles and lived there for fifty years. He published his first story in 1944, when he was twenty-four, and began writing poetry at the age of thirty-five. He died in San Pedro, California, on March 9, 1994, at the age of seventy-three, shortly after completing his last novel, *Pulp* (1994).

During his lifetime he published more than forty-five books of poetry and prose, including the novels *Post Office* (1971), *Ham on Rye* (1982), and *Hollywood* (1989). Among his most recent books are the posthumous editions of *What Matters Most Is How Well You Walk Through the Fire: New Poems* (1999), *Open All Night: New Poems* (2000), *Beerspit Night and Cursing: The Correspondence of Charles Bukowski and Sheri Martinelli, 1960–1967* (2001), *Night Torn Mad with Footsteps: New Poems* (2001), *sifting through the madness for the word, the line, the way: new poems* (2003), *The Flash of Lightning Behind the Mountain* (2004), *Slouching Toward Nirvana* (2005), *Come On In!* (2006), and *The People Look Like Flowers at Last* (2007).

All of his books have now been published in translation in more than a dozen languages and his worldwide popularity remains undiminished. In the years to come Ecco will publish additional volumes of previously uncollected poetry and letters.